LETHAL SECRET

The Seacastle Mysteries
Book 8

PJ Skinner

ISBN 978-1-913224-56-1

Copyright 2025 Parkin Press

Parkin Press
INDEPENDENT PUBLISHER

Cover design by Mariah Sinclair

Dedicated to my mother - the original cosy mystery fan in my family.
Her love, encouragement, and no-nonsense advice have always made everything seem possible.

Chapter 1

The sea churned brown in front of us as Harry Fletcher and I sat in the wind shelter near our terraced house. A brisk western wind whipped our trouser legs about but couldn't reach inside to the bench where we warmed our hands around our cups of strong tea. As I raised mine to my mouth, small ripples broke out on the surface.

'There's no need to blow on your tea here,' I said.

'Natural air conditioning,' said Harry. 'Hey, isn't that your buddy Herbert swooping in to see us?'

A large, intimidating herring gull landed near our feet with a plop of his pink ones. Herbert waddled up and down, staring at us with his gimlet eyes. He had matured into a rather scary, full-sized herring gull with a bright yellow beak marked with a red spot on the lower mandible. His pink legs appeared faintly silly under his robust body, but I didn't let him know that.

'I think he wants my crusts.'

'You'd better hand them over. He's got a beak, and he's not afraid to use it.'

I tore the edges off my bacon butty and threw them out to him. He tilted his head back and chorused in triumph before gobbling them up in double quick time. I never understood why seagulls advertised the presence of food before they'd eaten their fill. Their excitement at discovering food seemed to overwhelm them.

'Daft bird,' said Harry. 'A prime example of cupboard love.'

'Google says seagulls have an excellent memory for faces.'

'A good memory for suckers, more like. Can I have some more tea, please?'

We sat there for another five minutes, absorbing the ozone and gazing out at the wind farm. The turbines were working overtime in the stiff breeze as a large tanker chugged past on its way to Rotterdam.

'Ready?' said Harry.

We got back into our van and inserted a cassette into the deck, a relic from Harry's old van, which played our collection of tapes from the eighties and nineties. We passed by hedges laden with blossom and trees dotted with new lime green leaves. The traffic was light, and the journey made shorter by singing along to some of our favourite songs from Free's Greatest Hits. Soon we were arriving at the outskirts of Hove where we had a house clearance to complete. I felt a frisson of anticipation zip around my body as we pulled up to an Edwardian semi-detached house reached by a path of paving stones overgrown with dandelions and other tenacious weeds. A young man sat on the front step, his eyes red with a recent bout of weeping. He stood up to receive us, holding out a bunch of keys. He would not come inside the house with us. He gesticulated forlornly at the interior.

'I won't go in again. I expected her to be here, somehow, to feel her presence, to comfort me. But she's gone. Completely. It's so empty it hurts.'

'But she owned some outstanding pieces. Are you sure you won't take any of them as keepsakes?' I said.

'I already removed what I wanted. The rest are just pointless things. I don't care about them. Take them all.'

'I'm sorry for your loss,' said Harry. 'What would you like me to do with the keys?'

'Just post them through the letter box. Anything you leave is going to the junk yard anyway. People are welcome to steal something that takes their eye.'

He sloped off down the path, enveloped in grief, and turned onto the pavement, his hands shoved into his trouser pockets. He walked with his head down and his shoulders slumped. Soon he had disappeared from view. Harry shrugged.

'I guess we'd better get on with it then.'

The house contained an impressive assortment of treasures, the good, the bad and the downright tat, and it kept us busy for most of the day. At one stage, I walked to the local branch of Tesco and bought us some pork pies, cheese and onion crisps, and a bunch of seedless red grapes. I also picked up two lattes from the local coffee shop. We ate lunch sitting in the Parker Knoll his and hers armchairs with the slightly scuffed armrests and the saggy springs. The Wade ornaments stared at us accusingly from the mantlepiece, as if daring us to put them in the charity shop box. I felt profoundly sorry for the young man and his loss. Nobody tells the truth about death. They are so afraid of saying the word, they now use pass instead. We need to become accustomed to talking about it again. We are all dying. Some are dying faster than others, but none can escape.

After lunch, I ventured upstairs and emptied the wardrobes. To my surprise, I found two genuine flapper dresses in the wardrobe in a protective bag. I knew exactly who would give her right arm for these.

Maybe her left arm too. Grace Wong, who ran the Asian Antique Emporium with her husband Max, down the High Street from my vintage furniture shop, Second Home. I imagined her face as I casually unzipped the bag and took them out. There would be squeals of delight.

'What are you grinning at?' said Harry. 'Help me disassemble these beds. I can take them up to London to my cousin's warehouse if you don't want them. There's hardly anything in the house we can't sell. It's a great haul.'

We lumbered up and down the stairs at least a dozen times each before we had finished clearing the bedrooms. I found nothing of startling value in the house, but plenty of stock which would freshen up the content of my shop and find a new use with one of my clients. Lesser objects would get repurposed by Harry's cousin in London, with few left for kindling. I found one rather nice, slightly moth-eaten vintage Persian carpet in the spare room. I could picture it in our bedroom in the Grotty Hovel, our pet name for our house. It needed a dose of insecticide to kill the moth eggs first though, a job I hated.

By the time we finished and dropped the keys through the letterbox, evening approached.

'Do you fancy having fish and chips in the pub?' I asked.

'That sounds wonderful. I'll be your designated driver if you'd like a pint of cider.'

'If it's okay with you, I'll drive and you can have a drink. I'm gasping for a pot of tea.'

'Excellent. The Dog and Duck awaits. We can leave the van in the car park.'

The Dog and Duck heaved with office workers, tossing down a quick drink before going home. We searched in vain for a table and were about to leave when I spotted DI Terry Antrim sitting on his own in a corner snug. He worked at the Brighton police station and used to be a massive rival of my ex-husband DI George Carter's, but since working on some cases together they had become firm friends, each appreciating the other's abilities. As we approached the table, he looked up from his tablet and a broad grin spread over his skull like features. He had often reminded me of a praying mantis in a suit, being stick thin with long rebellious limbs which always seemed to be awkwardly folded.

'Tanya? How wonderful to see you! And Harry, of course.'

'Of course,' muttered Harry, who was well aware of DI Antrim's minor crush on me.

'Do you mind if we join you? We've just finished clearing out a house and we're starving.'

'I'd be delighted. I was about to eat as well. Here's the menu.'

He handed it to Harry, but he stared at me, making me feel quite shy.

'We've already chosen,' said Harry, handing it back. 'Let's order.'

'You need to go to the bar to order here,' said Terry. 'Do you mind awfully getting mine too? I'm hemmed in here.'

I could see from his face Harry minded quite a lot, but his natural good manners surfaced, and he smiled.

'Look after Tanya for me. I'll fight my way through the crowds.'

An exaggeration. In my experience, any crowd parted in front of Harry, like the Red Sea in front of the Israelites. His physical presence guaranteed respect. The military air he still gave off made other men jealous or wary. They always backed down if he puffed out his chest. Personally, I found his square bald head and muscular body a turn-on. Few men of his age looked better. Terry Antrim was almost his polar opposite, but his quiet dignity and ferocious intelligence won most arguments. I turned to Terry and smiled.

'Got any cases you need help with?'

He shook his head, but he couldn't help smiling back.

'None that I'm willing to tell you about, cheeky baggage. Police work is for professionals, although we are dealing with an odd case…'

He trailed off. I knew he wanted me to beg, and I wasn't strong enough to resist the temptation.

'Really? Please tell me about it. I promise to keep schtum.'

He beamed and rubbed his long, skinny hands together. I noticed the immaculate manicure and felt self-conscious about my torn cuticles and scratched hands. Hades, our rescue cat, still graced me with the odd scratch despite now tolerating the occasional snuggle with me. I put up with him, because he loved us all, especially my stepson Mouse. I leaned in to hear Terry over the competing voices and raucous laughter in the pub.

'We had an emergency call out at a care home, The Haven, this morning. They'd found a man dead in his chair. They told me it had been unexpected. It certainly didn't appear mysterious. After all, he was eighty-eight and had a terrible smoker's cough according to the nurse. But then I noticed the tiny veinlets in his eyes and the discarded pillow on the floor. He also had a broken finger.'

'Someone murdered him?'

'So it seems. But who tortures and murders a defenceless old man with mild dementia?'

'The torture sounds like an attempt to extract information, or to force him to sign something. A will? But why murder him? Frustration perhaps?'

'You mean perhaps the murderer didn't get what he was searching for? Hmm. You have a point. Anyway, the nurse told me he had talked about family in Seacastle in the past, but nobody ever came to visit him. I might ask George to check if he can find anyone who knew him. We're going to check the CCTV from the parking area outside the care home too. A middle-aged, dark-haired man was spotted before the attack, but nobody had a good look at him. The recording from the carpark may help. If we find anything useful, I'll let George know.'

'Why don't you text me the dead man's name and a photograph and I'll see if Roz can spread the news?'

'Ah, I remember, Foghorn? Wasn't that her nickname?'

He grinned.

'Whose nickname?' said Harry, arriving back at the table with a tray containing two pints of Spitfire beer and a pot of tea for me.

'Thanks, darling. We were talking about Roz.'

'Blimey, good job I interrupted you. I'm sure Terry would rather talk about the new cricket season.'

Terry winked at me.

'Quite right too,' he said.

Chapter 2

The next morning, I readied myself for the day at the shop with renewed optimism. The town of Seacastle had returned to a deep slumber after the departure of the Sloane Rangers reality show. Its citizens heaved a sigh of relief and returned to moaning about the weather and the price of heating their homes. They had finally paid me for my consultancy work at Sloane Rangers, but the reduced cheque would not keep the wolves from the door of the Grotty Hovel. Leaving home to serve non-existent customers in my vintage furniture shop did not appeal in the slightest. Only my natural optimism kept me slogging there through the wind and sleet, hoping to sell a six-pound lampshade or a battered sea-chest. Now, hope blossomed in my chest. Fresh stock would encourage people to browse the shop.

The Seacastle winter gave way to spring with all the grace of a bolshy businessman relinquishing his seat to a pregnant woman. Spring heralded its approach with a ferocious bout of westerly storms. The winds rampaged along the promenade and up the side streets to our terrace of houses. Every time a snowdrop forced its way to the surface in the back garden of the Grotty Hovel, the wind tried to tear it from its moorings in fury at its presumption. Hades refused to venture outside, unless forced to by the call of nature. I watched him like a hawk for signs he might choose a dark corner of the house instead, but his fastidious nature would not allow him to despoil his den. I empathised with him, staring at the cat flap, girding his loins to go outside, as I wrapped myself in my almost floor-length down coat and put on my hat and gloves. I heard the cat flap swing as I pulled the door shut behind me.

As I turned left to walk to work, I caught sight of our neighbour, Gladys Fitch, behind a twitching curtain. I gave her a cheery wave, but she looked straight through me. She had been behaving oddly since losing her lodger, Daisy Kallis. I wondered if it had affected her more than I realised. Harry and I had discussed dragging her for a drink at the Shanty pub and trying to extract her secrets with several hot toddies, but Gladys could be as silent as a grave when the mood took her. I might persuade her under the guise of a communal night out.

The wind blew me along the promenade past piles of seaweed torn from the seabed and chucked on the pebbles by the angry seas. Ahead of me, I could see the pier, which had been shored up by heavy duty scaffolding after a powerful storm had damaged the Victorian pilings. I had spent a cold half an hour feeding Herbert, the seagull, on bacon rinds and crusts of toast while I watched the heavy machinery struggle to get the temporary structures in place before the tide came in again.

I had chosen a break in the weather to walk to the shop, but sharp needles of sleet soon gave my face unwanted acupuncture. I turned into King's Street, grateful for shelter from the painful shower and headed towards Second Home. My shop had an old-fashioned wooden front like many others on the High Street. The deep red paint had peeled from the frames, and I noticed with irritation a long streak of seagull faeces on the upstairs window. I fought a running battle to keep the glass clean so customers in the Vintage café could look down on the street. To my surprise, Ryan Wells sat outside in his wheelchair, waiting for me to open. The landlord of the Shanty pub smiled shyly at me as I approached, screwing up his eyes behind his thick glasses.

'Hi there,' I said. 'We rarely see you outside the Shanty. I thought your powers would diminish if you were cut off from the source of your strength.'

'Like Samson?' he said, grinning. 'Don't worry. I gave my batteries a full charge before I left.'

'What are you doing here?'

'Shopping. Even spies have to buy birthday presents, you know.'

'It's Joy's birthday soon?'

He bit his lip.

'Today, actually, she's due back from Budapest this afternoon. Please don't tell her I left it until the last minute again, or she may ship me off to Siberia.'

'Your secret's safe with me.'

I opened the door and held it open while Ryan manoeuvred his chair inside.

'Will you have a rummage while I switch on the oil heater? It's brass monkeys in here, as Harry would say.'

Ryan beamed at me.

'I bet you don't know where that phrase came from,' he said.

'I thought I did, but I'm probably wrong. Enlighten me over a coffee. What would you like?'

'A latte, please.'

I saw him glance upstairs to the Vintage Café.

'A latte it is. Do you want any cake?'

'No, but if Ghita left you any whole cakes, I'll take one home for Joy's birthday.'

'There's a tipsy cherry cake.'

'Perfect.'

'Have a pootle around and I'll bring them down. We can use the painted table at the front to enjoy our coffees.'

'Are you sure? I'm loath to interrupt your work.'

I laughed.

'You're the only client. I think we'll be okay. We use tables from the stock upstairs as well. I'm only sorry the café isn't accessible. I simply can't afford it right now.'

'Oh, don't worry about that I'm used to it. I could install a lift if you wanted. We could fit it beside the staircase.'

'Really? That would be fantastic. Would it be expensive?'

'The materials are clogging up the cellar in the Shanty, so I'd be glad to get rid of them. I'll ponder on the design and get back to you.'

As Ryan made his way around the ground floor, picking up and replacing treasures of every era, I made us both coffees and put Ghita's creation in a box. My friend Ghita Chowdhury had an eclectic selection of jobs, which included helping me in the shop, cooking in the Surfusion restaurant across the road and making the most delicious cakes in Seacastle. She also ran our fitness group, the Fat Fighters, prone to random meet ups with eighties disco music and replenishing gossips with cake. She and Roz Murray were my best friends, and together we were more than formidable. Joy, Ryan's wife, joined in when she could, but, like Ryan, she was often out of the country on mysterious missions for the government. Ryan had once confessed to me that his injury had been caused during one which failed. He had sworn me to secrecy. I'm pretty good at secrets, although normally at getting them out of people, rather than keeping them to myself.

I placed the coffees on the table. Ryan pulled his towards him and took a cautious sip.

'Wonderful,' he said. 'Just what the doctor ordered to warm me up a tad. That reminds me of the brass monkeys. Did you know the original phrase came from a brass structure used by the navy to hold cannon balls? It was referred to as a monkey. When the temperature plummeted, the brass would contract, causing the iron balls to fall out.'

He gave me an impish grin.

'So, nothing to do with—'

'Nothing at all.'

I laughed.

'You must tell Harry. I'm sure he doesn't know this piece of lore. What are you doing for Joy's birthday, apart from the cake?'

'She doesn't like a lot of fuss.'

'So, nothing then?'

He nodded.

'Hey, why don't we all turn up at the Shanty tonight and surprise her? You can pretend you didn't know.'

He polished his glasses with his napkin.

'That would be splendid. She might even enjoy it.'

'I'll round up the troops then. Did you find anything that took your eye present-wise?'

'Joy collects many oddities, such as candlesticks, lacework, Byzantine art. I searched on the internet, but I couldn't find anything there. The truth is, I'm completely out of my depth. Joy is so stylish and I'm well…'

'Not? No offence.'

We both laughed. Joy liked to dress up in nineteen-fifties style dresses, like a housewife in a cigarette commercial, a style totally at odds with her daring work overseas. She wore her hair in the typical demi-wave of the era. She liked a sneaky cigarette, a habit I presumed Ryan had also noticed, although knowing him, he had not mentioned it to her. Ryan spun his chair around and headed for the rear of the shop.

'I noticed a rather unusual icon hanging on the back wall. It's right up her street. What do you know about it?'

'Ah, yes, not much really. I found it at a local car boot sale some months ago. It's painted on copper, and I suspect it may be valuable, but I haven't located an expert to give it a once over yet.'

'Is it for sale? Joy would love it.'

'I wouldn't know what to charge for it. A man who dropped in yesterday got quite excited about it, but I fobbed him off with the same excuse.'

'Why don't you lend it to me for tonight and we'll organise an expert later? I promise to pay you fair value, if I can afford it.'

'It's a deal.'

Chapter 3

Ryan's unexpected news about Joy's birthday party caused a flurry of activity amongst our friends' group. I texted Roz and Ghita, followed by Grace and Max Wong, the owners of the Asian Antique Emporium, the high-end competition to Second Home. Gladys agreed to come to the Shanty only after Harry knocked on her door and metaphorically twisted her arm. Rohan and Kieron, the owners of the Surfusion restaurant had a previous engagement, but my sister Helen promised to turn up too. Everyone liked Joy and Ryan. Their stewardship of the Shanty had converted it into the heart of Seacastle, a place for laughter, friendship and the occasional small-town drama. Their constant absences from England were a standing joke, but I remained the only person in town who knew the truth behind the rumours.

    We booked a taxi and travelled to the Shanty with Gladys who seemed more subdued than ever despite the prospect of a jolly evening with friends. The taxi dropped us in the car park, and we took the path along the bluff to the pub. The pub stood out against the dark night sky with its white walls and light emitting from its small windows, enticing people into its cosy interior. We entered and looked around. Few people had ventured out on a cold dark Tuesday, but Roz and her husband Ed were already seated in our favourite spot. Behind the bar, Ryan sat in his modified wheelchair, raised up so he could easily pull pints and chat to the customers. I caught his eye, and he shook his head.

'She's not here yet. I expected her to arrive by now. Her flight must be delayed again. I expect she'll turn up soon.'

He could not hide the tension in his voice. I wondered how much worry was mixed in with his disappointment. They had always led this peculiar existence together, but the dangers must have loomed larger since Ryan had been shot.

'That's a pity, mate,' said Harry. 'Why don't you let Shaylah take over the bar and have a drink with us for a change?'

Ryan glanced at Shaylah flicking her hair from side to side and pouting. He rolled his eyes at Harry and they both snorted.

'Great idea. Let me get the drinks in first.'

Soon, we were all sitting in the nook with our drinks. The pub had a natural cosy feeling conducive to long natters and missed curfews. The thick stone walls kept in the heat no matter the weather outside, and the small doors and windows contributed to the locked-in atmosphere. Ryan and Joy had renovated the pub, rescuing it from a filthy shell to a cosy seaside pub with walls decorated by paintings of stormy seas and fisherman's ephemera like lists of the month's catch. Glass fisherman's globes dangled from the ceiling among scraps of netting. Wooden tables and snugs lined in deep red and green velvet invited long leisurely stays. Joy had also put together a fantastic menu of typical pub grub. Harry was partial to her steak and kidney pies, and we often had lunch there together at the weekend.

We had been joined by Helen and Ghita who were embroiled in a passionate discussion about baking. Helen had taken out her phone and was tapping away, storing one of Ghita's highly prized recipes. Roz looked up as I approached with the drinks and cleared space at the table.

'You seem to have organised a birthday party without a birthday girl,' she said, grinning. 'Or did Joy refuse to come?'

'She's probably delayed at the airport,' said Ryan, gliding up to our table in his chair. 'She won't be long.'

'Great,' said Ed. 'I'm dying for a slice of the tipsy cherry cake. I think it's my absolute favourite.'

We had all downed our drinks and were telling our favourite stories about the Shanty when a commotion occurred outside. Shaylah burst through the door.

'There's somebody lying on the grass near the path,' she said, gasping for breath. 'And they're not moving.'

Ryan's face drained of blood in an instant and I felt my stomach clench with fear. Everyone stared at him, unable to avoid jumping to conclusions.

'Stay calm, everyone,' he said. 'Harry, can you please go outside and investigate with Tanya? There's a torch behind the bar. I'll call the ambulance.'

Harry jumped up, puffing out his chest.

'No problem,' he said. 'I completed advanced first aid training during my days in the army. Come with me, Tanya.'

We followed Shaylah outside. Her mascara had run down her cheeks, and she looked like a member of a Goth band. She grabbed my arm as we reached the door, sniffling.

'I didn't want to tell Ryan, but I think it's Joy lying there.'

'Are you sure?'

'No, but it's pitch black out.'

I gathered myself.

'Stay here and stop people from leaving.'

'Me? But I can't.'

'It's important. If she has been attacked, the suspect may be in the pub. Do your best.'

I hurried after Harry, almost tripping in the dark and took a moment to steady myself and lower my heart rate. I started down the path and caught sight of him bending over a shape lying on the ground a short distance into the grass.

He turned to face me, his expression grim in the torchlight.

'Don't come close. It's not a pretty sight. Somebody has bludgeoned them about the head, and we must preserve the forensic evidence.'

I whispered, 'Are they dead?'

'I think so, but I can't be certain. She may have been attacked. There's a lot of blood. We should call the police.'

I could hardly get the next word out.

'She?'

He nodded.

'I can't be sure, but I think it may be Joy. It's so dark and there is so much blood I can't see her clearly.'

'Oh no. What about Ryan?'

'He'll have to be told. They might need a DNA sample to identify her. A hairbrush or something like that. Can you help the ambulance crew to locate me? Use the torch on your phone. It's pitch black along the path.'

I nodded and headed for the car park. As soon as I reached it, I rang George. He's not only my ex-husband. He's also the local detective inspector and my sister Helen's boyfriend (it's a long story).

'Tan? What's up? Is Helen okay? I thought the party would continue for hours yet. I was planning on dropping by to kiss the birthday girl later.'

'Helen's fine. It's Joy. I think someone's attacked her on her way to the Shanty.'

My voice caught in my throat, and I choked back a sob. George's tone of voice changed in an instant, and I heard DI George Carter on the line.

'Stay right where you are. I'll pick up Flo and be with you shortly. Is Harry there with you?'

'Yes, He's guarding the body. There's a lot of blood. You'll need lights. It's pitch black out there.'

'Okay. Stay calm and keep people away from the site. Don't let anybody leave.'

'Shaylah, the bar girl, is preventing people from exiting the pub. I'm at the car park waiting for the ambulance.'

'Please tell them not to contaminate the scene. They should stick to the same route to approach the body. Tell them to lay a tarp on the ground if they can find one. Does Ryan know yet?'

'No.'

A long sigh.

'I suppose it was only a matter of time before their careers caught up with them,' he said.

'You knew about them?'

'Of course. Do you really think I'd missed the clues? Most people suspect them of spying. Anyway, we were advised of their presence by MI5 as a matter of courtesy. If she's really dead, Ryan will have to notify the spooks.'

'Do you think it's connected with their work?'

'I think you should stay out of this, Tan. It's way above our pay grade.'

'But Joy is our friend.'

'You don't know it's her. Let's identify the body first. I'm on the way. Try to prevent people trampling the crime scene if you can. We'll be there soon.'

Chapter 4

Once the paramedics had arrived and we had given them George's instructions, Harry and I returned to the Shanty. I shivered with cold and shock. Harry noticed and put his jacket around my shoulders.

'How will we tell Ryan?' I said. 'The news could kill him.'

'We can't be sure of the victim's identity. Ryan deserves to know the facts.'

'I guess so. I can't believe our lovely surprise party has turned into a crime scene. It was my idea. Joy might be dead because of me.'

Harry grabbed my shoulders and stared into my eyes.

'I need you to hold it together. This is not your business. Joy and Ryan are involved in matters we know nothing about. Ryan must cope with the results, no matter how horrible. Promise me?'

'I promise.'

We stumbled through the tiny door into a silent pub. Shaylah wept on Roz's shoulder and Ryan sat white-faced in his wheelchair waiting for us.

'Is it true?' he said, his voice catching in his throat. 'Is my Joy gone?'

'I can't say,' said Harry. 'They are taking a woman with serious injuries to the hospital. It's not possible to identify her yet.'

'But she looks like Joy?'

'She does. I'm so sorry mate.'

Ryan slumped in his chair. I wanted to hug him, but I wasn't sure if he would accept physical contact. He had always been slightly aloof and left the hugging to Joy. Perhaps he felt awkward in his chair. I had never asked Joy about it. The Ryan we knew loved technology and politics and sport, but he showed no inclination for close contact with us. Or was it us who held off? I wasn't sure. Desperation at the dreadful situation almost overwhelmed me. I felt Harry take my hand in his warm, callused one and my panic subsided. I glanced at him gratefully. The muscles in his cheeks were taut and bloodless. I squeezed his hand, grateful for his self-control.

'Sit down,' said Ryan. 'I don't imagine the police will allow us to leave yet. Shaylah, give everyone a drink on the house.'

Shaylah's eyes opened wide.

'I can't.'

'I can,' said Roz. 'Tanya, give me a hand behind the bar.'

Somehow, we refilled everyone's glasses, although I noticed most people had switched to coffee.

'In case the DI wants to question me,' said one man.

'Mine's a double. Did you see the body?' hissed a woman I didn't recognise.

I pretended I hadn't heard her and resisted the temptation to spit into her drink. Instead, I shoved it at her aggressively, hoping she would retreat.

As the last drinks were served, George and Flo entered the pub, eyes down, with solemn expressions on their faces. People made room for them to approach our table where Ryan sat strangely calm, waiting for news. George put his hand on Ryan's shoulder.

'The paramedics have removed the body,' he said. 'I'm afraid they couldn't save her.'

Ryan bit his lip.

'Can I go with them?'

George glanced at Flo, and she shook her head.

'They've taken her to the morgue,' she said. 'It's better to wait until we prepare the body.'

'There's nothing you can do for her now, except to give Flo something belonging to Joy, a hairbrush or a toothbrush. We'll get a DNA test done as soon as we can.'

Ryan blinked rapidly, and I thought he might cry. Instead, he nodded and directed his chair to the back of the pub. I stood to follow him, but Harry tugged at my sleeve.

'Let him do it. He's a private man. He may need a few minutes alone.'

I sat down again, conscious of the devastated expressions on our friends' faces. I pinched myself surreptitiously to make sure I was not having a nightmare.

'Now,' said George. 'Who's the young lady who found the body?'

Shaylah tore herself away from Roz.

'Me, your honour,' she said, shaking.

George smiled.

'There's no need for that. You can call me DI Carter. Let's sit in the snug and you can tell me what you saw. Okay?'

Shaylah sniffed loudly and followed him across the pub. Flo stayed with us. A tear slid down her cheek and she wiped it away with a velvet sleeve. The bun in her hair had slipped to one side, and she took out the kirby grips, holding it in place, before reassembling it. Grey tendrils hung around her face and she looked ten years older.

'I can't believe it,' she whispered. 'Joy, dead? It seems impossible. That woman had nine lives, from what I hear.'

'Are you sure it's her?' I asked. 'Joy was more than capable of defending herself.'

Harry raised an eyebrow.

'And how do you know that?'

I could feel all eyes on me as I searched for an answer. I lied.

'She's a black belt in Aikido.'

'Joy? Are you certain? I suppose she always seemed strong for her weight at Fat Fighters' box fit classes.'

I nodded.

'She looked as if she couldn't hurt a fly,' said Roz. 'Just goes to show how little we knew about her.'

'Don't talk about her in the past tense,' said Flo. 'We can't identify the body yet. The attack damaged the facial features…'

She trailed off as Ryan glided back into the pub, holding a Ziplock bag containing a tortoiseshell hairbrush, his eyes puffy. He didn't appear to have heard her, thank goodness.

'I've sealed it for them,' he said.

'Perfect.'

A loud sob broke the silence. I turned to see Gladys sitting in the corner, tears streaming down her face. She dabbed at them ineffectually with a tiny lace handkerchief. As far as I knew, Gladys and Joy had rarely met, but Gladys appeared to be heartbroken. I made my way over to her and sat beside her on the banquette.

'Are you all right?'

She shook her head and turned away.

'Leave me alone. You don't understand.'

I wanted to question her further, but George appeared, followed by a downcast Shaylah, who returned to the comfort of Roz's arms. George shrugged at me. I sympathised. I couldn't imagine Shaylah being much of a witness. She struggled to remember a round of drinks. George tapped Ryan's arm.

'Do you feel up to answering some questions, Mr Wells? Or we could do this later?'

'No, it's all right. I'll do it now. Can Tanya come with me? She's the only one who knows about us.'

I thought George would refuse, but he crooked his finger at me, and we headed for the snug.

'Can you take notes please, Tan?'

'I can record it on my phone too, if you like?'

'Okay, but you must send it to Joe Brennan and delete the original when he gives you the word. Flo, can you and the girls make a list of all the customers in the pub with their names and addresses, please?'

I saw Roz's jaw drop.

'You want us to help?' said Ghita.

'That's what I said.'

I avoided their eyes and tried not to smirk. George did not encourage our participation in his investigations, even though we had helped him solve a few of his cases. We walked to the snug, made gloomy by a blown lightbulb, the dark sky outside adding to the foreboding atmosphere. Ryan parked his wheelchair as close to the table as it would go. George leaned forward and patted his forearm.

'I understand today is Joy's birthday. I'm terribly sorry. This must be a dreadful shock.'

'She's not dead though,' said Ryan.

'Well,' said George, looking uncomfortable. 'We aren't sure it's her, but Flo says it's likely.'

Ryan seemed to smile. His change of mood shocked me.

'I'd know if she was dead. She's alive.'

George shifted in his seat.

'Be that as it may, I need to get my facts straight.'

'Fire away.'

I almost laughed. Since he had gone to collect the brush, Ryan seemed to have travelled to a different dimension on a different timeline. Perhaps he knew something we didn't. Why didn't he believe Joy had been murdered? And why had Gladys reacted so strongly? My mind whirled. George coughed, bringing me back to the present.

'Can you tell me what Joy was doing in Budapest? I presume she travelled there for work?' said George.

'Work? Oh no. It wasn't a mission. Or not one I knew about.' He scratched his head. 'I can't imagine they kept me out of the loop…'

'Did she tell you what she would be doing?'

'No. She told me it was a secret. She seemed excited, though.'

'What time did she arrive in England?'

Ryan fidgeting in his chair.

'Um, well, I can't say. She might still be sitting in a plastic chair in Budapest airport or even be back at her hotel.'

'Assuming she arrived in Britain, could someone have followed her home?'

Ryan chuckled.

'Absolutely impossible. No one could follow Joy without her knowing. Not even me. She had a sixth sense about that.'

'Did she have any enemies?' said George.

'A fair few.'

George swallowed. His cheeks had turned pink.

'Can you narrow that down?'

'Not really. It depends which country you are talking about.'

'How about here in Britain?'

'Now? I'm not sure. Most returned home to Russia and Eastern Europe years ago. Even the embedded spies. Until recently, there wasn't any point wasting resources on having spies in Britain. I don't know anyone who wanted to hurt her.'

George sighed.

'When did she last contact you?'

'A few hours ago.'

'What did she say?'

'She told me she would lie low for a while because someone had been stalking her.'

'But you don't know who?'

'No.'

'Okay, I'll need you to come down to the station tomorrow to identify the body. Can I send a squad car to collect you?'

'No, I've got transport. Just text me when you are ready.'

Chapter 5

Dawn was breaking by the time the police released the clientele of the Shanty. Flo, who seemed shellshocked by the night's events, gave Harry, Gladys and me a lift home. She dropped us off outside our adjoining terraced houses. Gladys let herself in without a word, her face swollen with sorrow. I didn't want to leave her alone, but she wouldn't talk to me. We climbed the stairs, weary from our ordeal and got ready for bed. Lazy pink clouds hovered over the eastern horizon, which glowed orange through the windows of the Grotty Hovel. Hades had made himself at home in our bed and made his objections known when we tried to turf him onto the floor.

'He thinks he's the head of the family,' said Harry.

'He certainly eats better than anyone else. His gourmet food costs a fortune.'

We lay in bed with Hades restored to his rightful place on the covers and failed to sleep. The sun peeped in the window to find us still awake. I tried to understand the night's events, but without context I could only begin to process the shock. I could almost hear Harry fighting with his internal doubts. Finally, he turned over to face me.

'Why didn't you tell me the truth about Ryan and Joy?' he said, raising himself on one elbow. 'You tell me everything. Even women's stuff I don't want to know about.'

I shrugged.

'Ryan made me swear not to tell anyone. He only told me as a protective measure in case they disappeared one day.'

'But spies? I thought the speculation about them was silly local gossip.'

'So did I. Until Ryan confided in me.'

Harry frowned.

'Could a foreign spy have murdered Joy?'

'We don't know it's her.'

'I saw her up close, though. I know it was dark, but it sure looked like Joy.'

'We should know today. Poor old Ryan has to identify the body.'

'Did you notice Gladys weeping in the corner during the police interviews?'

'I did. I thought it was odd considering how seldom she comes to the pub. It's not like she knows Joy and Ryan well.'

'Do you think she has depression? She's been behaving strangely lately. I can't get a smile out of her anymore,' I said.

'You're the expert. I'm not great at feelings.'

'You do okay,' I said, kissing him. 'I might knock on her door and ask if she wants a cuppa.'

Harry kissed me back and turned over. A few moments later, I heard a gentle snore from his side of the bed. I snuggled up to his back and soon I slept too.

The smell of bacon woke me several hours later. I wrapped myself in my dressing gown and staggered downstairs to find Harry making bacon buttys in the kitchen. He had laid the table and made a pot of tea. My mouth watered at the thought of breakfast.

'Shall I invite Gladys in for a butty?' I asked.

'Sure, there's plenty, but Hades may lose out.'

'He'll have to be brave.'

I slipped out onto the street and knocked on Gladys's door. She took her time to arrive, also in her dressing gown. Her hair had a just-out-of-bed look and her eyes sported black bags.

'Morning,' I said. 'We thought you might fancy a bacon butty.'

'I don't have the strength to resist,' she said. 'Do you mind if I come in my nighty? I haven't got dressed yet.'

'You'll fit right in,' I said, twirling around in my pyjamas.

She shuffled into our house, looking a hundred years old, and sniffing the air like a bloodhound. Harry pulled out a chair for her in the kitchen and poured her a cup of strong tea. She sipped it cautiously and shrank into her chair like a shy white raisin.

'Ketchup or brown sauce?' said Harry.

'Oh, brown sauce, please,' she said.

Harry placed a butty in front of her and then me, before sitting down himself.

'Bon appetite,' he said, waving his sandwich in the air and dislodging a blob of brown sauce which landed on the table.

Gladys emitted a choking sound, which may have been a laugh. She nibbled on her sandwich and a little colour came back to her cheeks. I ate mine in big bites, feeling the butter running down my chin. Harry leaned over and dabbed at me with a napkin.

'Honestly, woman, what a mess! I'm going to have to buy you a bib.'

'These are delicious,' said Gladys, licking her lips. 'I didn't realise how hungry I was.'

'Harry is well trained,' I said.

'Unlike you,' he said.

I grinned at him, and we finished our sandwiches in silence. Gladys wiped her mouth with her napkin and pushed her chair back from the table.

'Don't go,' I said. 'Last night affected us all, but you worried me with your sobbing fit. I hate to pry, but can you tell us what's wrong?'

Gladys grimaced.

'It's not something I wanted to discuss yet, but you'll find out soon enough about my DNA and all that.'

I wasn't at all sure I'd heard her correctly. Was she admitting to murdering Joy?

'DNA?' said Harry. 'Why would your DNA be involved?'

'It's on file with the police. They took it during the murder inquiry for Cyril Prout.'

'You've lost me, Gladys. Why is your DNA relevant to the murder? Should we contact George?' I asked.

'Oh, I imagine he'll contact me. It's too late, you see. I should've done something sooner. I'll never forgive myself.'

Gladys sobbed as if her heart had been torn out. Harry looked at me for guidance. I put my hand on her knee.

'Gladys? What on earth is going on?'

'My daughter has been murdered.'

'Your daughter? You didn't tell us you had a daughter. Why didn't you say anything?'

'Because I was ashamed of giving her away. I only found her recently, but I waited too long. She's gone, and I never had the chance to tell her how much I loved her.'

Harry slapped his forehead.

'Joy? Joy Wells is your daughter?'

Gladys nodded. I felt my heart sink. I couldn't think of anything to say as she sat weeping in my kitchen chair. What can you say to a grieving mother, especially one who has lost the daughter she has found after fifty years apart? Tears escaped from my eyes and ran hot down my cheeks. I crouched down beside Gladys's chair and held her in my arms. Her sobs tore through the silence in the kitchen, making almost physical rents in the atmosphere. Harry bit his lip and tried not to cry too.

Suddenly, my phone rang, making us all jump. Harry picked it up.

'It's Flo,' he said, thrusting it towards me. 'You'd better take it.'

I released Gladys, who sat small and tragic in her chair, and took it from him. I cleared my throat and took the call.

'Flo? Have you got news about the murder?'

'Yes, but you're not going to believe it.'

'Tell me.'

'The victim is not Joy Wells. Ryan told us to check for a livid scar on her back, but the victim didn't have one. However, she is almost identical to Joy, perhaps a little younger. It's hard to tell because of her injuries. We've sent some samples for rush genetic testing. We should get the results soon.'

I gasped and caught Gladys staring at me.

'What now?' said Harry.

'Does Ryan know Joy is still alive?' I asked.

'Yes, he's here at the station.'

'Has he heard from Joy yet?'

'No, she's disappeared. Her phone is off too. I've got to go. George is on the war path.'

I hung up to find Glady staring at me, her eyes shining.

'Joy is still alive?'

'As far as we know, but the murder victim is almost identical to Joy, so they are doing DNA analysis.'

'Sandor had more children?'

'Who's Sandor?' said Harry.

'It's a long story,' said Gladys.

'I'll make another pot of tea,' he said.

Chapter 6

In the end, we got dressed first, as Gladys felt uncomfortable telling us her life story while still in her night gown. We agreed to reconvene in her house so she could dig out some photographs for us. Harry and I climbed upstairs to have a shower and get ready. I almost fell out of the shower in my haste to wash and go. I watched Harry dry his toes one by one with great care before he put his socks on. This habit originated from his days in the army, when keeping his feet in good condition for 'yomping' had been vital, so I held back any sarky comments about his lack of urgency. I had thrown on my clothes while my hair still dripped on the carpet and now attempted to dry it by dabbing ineffectually. I forced a brush through the tangles left by skipping conditioner in my rush to be ready.

'Honestly,' said Harry, watching me struggle. 'She won't thank us for rushing her. I bet she's going through her possessions looking for the relevant photographs.'

He was right, of course. Gladys had her own way of doing things, and we needed to respect it no matter how much I yearned to immerse myself in this new mystery. He plugged in my hairdryer.

'Sit on the bed and I'll give it a quick blast. It's chilly out there this morning. You don't want to catch your death of cold.'

He sounded just like my mother, but I didn't object. I sat meekly on the corner while he brushed and dried my hair, whistling tunelessly, which he did when he felt content. He loved to brush my hair, as he knew how much pleasure I got from the smooth strokes massaging my scalp. We had become even closer after he told me the truth about Afghanistan and the invisible barrier between us had melted. I gave a tiny moan of pleasure and Harry laughed.

'You're worse than Hades,' he said. 'You'll be pestering me to open a tin of rabbit soon.'

My phone pinged, preventing me from replying. A message from Gladys. *Come when you are ready.* Harry wound the cord around the handle of the dryer and put it back in the drawer while I pulled on my pixie boots. I used the mirror to put on some lipstick and admired my silky locks.

'Thank you, sweetheart. My hair looks great.'

Harry grinned and spun me around to face him.

'You should have kissed me before putting on your lipstick. Now I'm going to have to smudge it.'

A couple of minutes later, with me wearing a newly applied layer of lipstick, we popped next door to Gladys's house, making sure Hades didn't follow us. He had taken to visiting Gladys, but always through the back garden. Hades had no experience with traffic, and I lived in terror of him running out into the road. Gladys opened the door and let us into her dining room. She had placed an old photograph album and some paper files on the table. To my surprise, she also produced an iPad and started scrolling on it before putting it beside the other items.

'Would you like some tea?' she asked.

'No thanks,' said Harry. 'I'm still sloshing about after my two mugs at breakfast.'

She smiled and sat down opposite us. Her eyes were misty with unshed tears.

'I'm going to tell you everything Mouse discovered about me,' she said. 'I finally found out where I came from before my adoption. Have you heard of the Cook sisters?'

I shook my head, and Harry did the same.

'They were born in Sunderland but moved down to Battersea in London as young women to work for the civil service for two pounds a week as secretaries. They were unmarried women, typical of their time, left without partners after the slaughter of the Great War. One evening, Louise attended a talk about opera, where they played the audience extracts from famous arias, and she fell instantly in love with the music. She and Ida scraped together the princely sum of twenty-three pounds to buy a gramophone with ten LPs of their favourite operas. They listened to them constantly and soon had a favourite soprano, Amelita Galli-Curci. They bought tickets to see her sing at the Royal Opera house and afterwards they were hooked. They planned a trip to New York to see her perform again and scrimped and saved for a year to travel third class by ship. Ida had sent an embroidered handkerchief to Galli-Curci telling her about the trip, and to their great joy, she sent them tickets to watch her perform and they were invited to her home to meet her. When they got home to Britain, Ida wrote an article about their trip which was accepted by Mabs magazine. She was invited to write more articles for the magazine and eventually branched out into romance with brilliant success. Mills and Boon, who published romantic pulp fiction, offered her a contract to write books for them. Under the name of Mary Burchell, Ida wrote one hundred and thirty romantic novels. This earned her the bonanza wages of one thousand pounds a year, and soon the sisters were travelling all over Europe, watching opera. They became well known on the circuit because of their enthusiasm and made lots of friends among the impresarios and stars of the shows.'

'But how are they connected with you?' I asked.

'Patience is a virtue,' said Gladys, clearing her throat. 'Around the start of World War Two, one of their new friends. Viorica Ursuleac, an Austrian soprano, told them about the plight of Jewish people under the Nazi regime. Those who wished to emigrate were forced to abandon their belongings, but they had to meet the financial thresholds to enter Britain. Louise and Ida hit on the idea of wearing the nest eggs of Jews fleeing from Europe disguised as fur coats and jewels. They risked their lives to cross the frontiers dressed as wealthy spinsters after entering by another route wearing only a tweed suit. They stayed in expensive hotels, often the same ones as Nazi officials, and swanned about dressed up to the nines. They saved twenty-nine people and helped rescue countless others who used their newly purchased flat at Dolphin Court.'

'I never heard of them before,' said Harry. 'They were heroines.'

'They were honoured as Righteous among the Nations by Yad Vashem in Israel. And more recently recognised as British Heros of the Holocaust. Weren't they amazingly brave?'

'Can you imagine what would have happened if the Nazis had caught them?' I asked. 'It doesn't bear thinking about. But how are you connected to them?'

'My real name is Miriam Steinberg. My parents, Jozsef and Erzsébet sent me to England from Budapest as a baby just before the start of the war. The Cook sisters smuggled their valuables to England so I could get a visa from the government. My parents planned to join me, but something went wrong, and they never arrived. I was taken in by a childless English couple, Mabel and Horace Fitch, who changed my name to Gladys. They were strict parents who expected me to look after them in their old age.' A mischievous grin lit up her face. 'Unfortunately for them, I had other ideas. Here's a photo of us, taken after the war.'

She slid a photograph across the table. It showed a young couple dressed in overcoats, sitting in deckchairs on the beach. The woman wore a headscarf tied under her chin and the man wore a knotted handkerchief over his bald head. A little girl in a spotted dress played on the sand. She appeared to be posing for the camera.

'I was quite a bombshell as a young woman, which didn't go unnoticed by my male peers,' said Gladys, passing us a photograph of her younger self with a cheeky expression on her face.

'You still are,' said Harry, winking at her.

'I could never resist a man in uniform,' she replied, pink with pleasure. 'That's where Sandor Sabyani comes into the picture. He came to London with his parents after Hungary fell behind the Iron Curtain. You can't imagine how handsome he was, especially in his cadet's uniform. All the girls fancied Sandor, but he only had eyes for me.'

'No surprise there,' I said. 'And you fell for him too?'

'My mother warned me about him and tried to stop him from coming to the house, but he wouldn't take no for an answer. She even sent me to secretarial college for a year, but she couldn't keep us apart. I married him on my twenty-first birthday.'

'How romantic.'

'It was, for a while, but when I fell pregnant, he lost interest in me and started staying out late. I knew he had other women. He didn't even bother to hide it. And then one night, he didn't come home. He never returned, and I soon ran out of money. I was forced to return home with my tail between my legs. Mabel took me in on condition I had the baby adopted "to give it a better chance at life". After a bitter fight, I gave in and moved back with the Fitches. It wasn't as if I had much choice. In that era, being divorced with a child cut off all possibility of a decent career. I made a tough choice for Joy, and for me, but as time went by, I came to regret my decision. I searched high and low for her, but she had disappeared into the archives and mothers had no rights to reconnect with their adopted children in those days.'

She sniffed and dabbed at her eyes with an embroidered handkerchief.

'How did you find her?' said Harry.

Gladys ignored his question and shuffled the photographs like a deck of cards.

'Gladys? What are you hiding?' I asked.

'I made him swear he wouldn't tell you,' she said.

Light dawned.

'Mouse? I should have known. You two were as thick as thieves during his last break from University.'

Harry raised his eyebrows at me. Mouse, real name Andrew Carter, was George's son from his first marriage. He had moved in with me after my divorce and never left. He had become my surrogate son. Harry and I adored him, and after a rocky start, he had reconciled with George, so much so he had gone to University to study forensic computing so he could join the police force. His ability to hack into any system was legendary. Trust Gladys to bring in the expert.

'You must have been stunned to find your daughter living so close by,' said Harry.

'But why didn't you tell Joy?' I asked.

'I wanted to, but I was afraid she might not understand about me giving her up. What if she didn't want me?' Her voice broke. 'And to think I almost lost her. I'm going to tell her the truth as soon as she gets home.'

I exchanged a glance with Harry. I could read his mind. If she gets home…

'Please keep me in the loop,' said Gladys. 'The station is as leaky as a sieve where you are concerned. I may be able to help.'

'I promise.'

Chapter 7

The next couple of days were agony for Gladys as no leads emerged regarding the whereabouts of Joy Wells or the identification of the murdered woman. Every time I left or entered my home, I could see her curtains twitching and her hopeful face appear. I shook my head at her, only to see her crestfallen expression return. Gladys was not alone in longing for news from the police station. Ghita and Roz were agog at the drama and hung out at the shop, hoping to pick up some news. But even Roz's famous antenna couldn't pick up any stray gossip about the murder. That didn't stop her from forming theories about the motives of some of the Shanty's customers that night. The fact George had asked her to help gather the names and addresses of the people present had gone to her head and she now fancied herself as Sherlock Holmes.

'I suspect the woman who ordered the double gin and tonic after the body had been found. She probably needed to calm down after bludgeoning the victim. I didn't trust her. She had shifty eyes, didn't she, Ghita?'

Ghita did not appreciate being relegated to the Dr Watson role.

'Honestly,' she muttered to me. 'Who does she think she is? You're the Jessica Fletcher of our group. Don't you have any clues we can follow up?'

'Not right now, but I need a slice of your excellent new cake to keep up my strength. Roz, can you nip to the Co-op to buy some milk?'

'Okay, but we need to discuss the dodgy woman. I'm sure it's her.'

Ghita and I went upstairs to the Vintage Café and made some shots of espresso. Ghita cut a slice of her newest creation and placed it before me on the table.

'Voila!'

'Wow! It looks fabulous. What flavour is it?'

'Chocolate orange. I based it on the Jaffa cake. It has orange flavoured sponge with orange butter icing between the layers and chocolate frosting on the top.'

'My mouth's watering at the thought.'

Roz trundled up the stairs with the milk.

'That looks wonderful. I can't wait to try it,' she said, pouring the milk into the jug for frothing.

She brought the lattes to the table and took a bite from her slice of cake.

'Oh my goodness. You are a genius, Ghita,' she said. 'How do you do it?'

Ghita blushed with pleasure, all resentment forgotten.

'I'm glad you like it. I wasn't sure it would work.'

'It works,' I said. 'I may have an orgasm on the spot.'

'Please don't,' she said, cringing.

We scoffed our cake and sipped our coffees in the quiet of the empty shop. Roz reached into her handbag and took out a mini speaker.

'I thought we could have music upstairs in the café,' she said.

'How does that work?' I said. 'Is that a radio?'

Roz and Ghita laughed at me.

'You're still a Luddite at heart,' said Roz. 'It works with Bluetooth. You just have to find it with your phone and connect it. Then you can play your music through the speaker.'

I didn't admit it, but my music was mostly on cassettes in our clearance van and CDs back at the Grotty Hovel.

'I'll watch,' I said.

As usual with technological matters, the theory couldn't have been simpler, but the reality turned out to be significantly more difficult. They spent at least half an hour trying to get first Roz's and then Ghita's phones to find the speaker. I tried not to smirk as they became more and more frustrated.

'I'm sweating with effort,' said Roz. 'Why did you switch it off again?'

'I didn't. It says Bluetooth is activated. The signals could interfere with each other. Switch yours off.'

'I have got mine off. Can you see the speaker on the Bluetooth list?'

'No, my phone can't find it.'

'Honestly, where's Mouse when you need him?'

'I'm so stressed. Why can't we do this?'

I bit my lip and tried not to gloat. Then my mobile phone alerted me to the arrival of a text. When I noticed George had sent it, all the hairs on my arms stood on end. I did not alert Ghita and Roz, but opened it as nonchalantly as I could: A summons to attend a meeting at the station.

'Um, I've got to go now. Can you two hold the fort until I return?'

'Where are you going?' said Roz. 'Is there news of the case?'

I swear she could be psychic sometimes.

'Possibly.'

Roz elbowed Ghita, who squeaked in indignation.

'She's going to the station.'

'Oh, please come back and tell us all the news,' said Ghita.

'I can't promise anything.'

I put on my coat and dashed out of the door before Roz could ask me any more questions. I set out at a trot but soon settled into a brisk walk. I may have given up smoking, apart from the odd emergency, but I'm still not famous for my stamina under speed. Grace Wong spotted me coming from the door of her posh antique emporium and tried to wave me down, but I refused to stop and swerved her feeble efforts with a shrug.

'Can't stop now. I'm late.'

'Are you going to the police station?'

'Whatever gave you that idea?'

'I know that purposeful cadence.'

But I had already passed her shop, lengthening my stride as my excitement increased. I arrived at the reception, panting with exertion. Sally Wright looked up from her screen and smiled at me.

'They're in the meeting room one. I'll buzz you in.'

I pushed my way through the security doors and made my way up the passage to the meeting room. Several of the veterans acknowledged my presence with a grin, no longer surprised at my appearances inside the station. George, Flo and Joe Brennan, his deputy waited for me inside the room. I didn't shake their hands, fearful of the jolt of static electricity that came with it.

'That was quick,' said George. 'You didn't have to run.'

'I didn't,' I said, trying to mask my heavy breathing. 'What's new?'

'We got the DNA results back from the lab,' said Flo.

'The dead woman is Joy's half-sister,' said Joe. 'Can you believe it?'

'What?'

My mind did cartwheels. Presumably Gladys had not given up a second child. Surely she would have told us? Sandor's behaviour suggested a more reasonable explanation for the existence of half-siblings. But what did she want with Joy? A family reunion, perhaps?

'On the father's side,' said George. 'The results suggest both of her parents are from Hungary, probably the Jewish community. And since the DNA on the hairbrush gave the same result…'

'Unfortunately, the attacker took her handbag so we couldn't get her ID yet,' said Joe.

I took a deep breath and blurted out my news.

'Her father's name is Sandor Sabyani. Or was. He might be dead, as he would be in his eighties.'

I could almost hear the communal thud of dropping jaws hitting the table. George guffawed.

'I give up. How the hell did you know that?'

'Gladys Fitch is Joy's mother, and she used to be married to Sandor.'

'Since when?' said Joe.

'Two days ago. I didn't know it was relevant until you told me the murdered woman was Joy's half-sister.'

'Well, isn't Gladys a dark horse?' said Flo. 'And you believe her?'

Joe coughed.

'We have her DNA on the system after we took it to eliminate her from our inquiries. We could check.'

'We need her permission,' said Flo.

George scratched his head.

'Joe, can you first check the data base for a Sandor Sabyani and any children? We'll wait.'

'I'll be right back.'

If my mind had been whirring before, it shot into overdrive. Did Ryan know about Joy's sister, or her arrival at the Shanty? Could Joy have bumped into her sibling outside? It would explain her disappearance, but why would she have killed her?

'This makes little sense,' said George. 'It would help if we had the killer's DNA.'

'No luck so far,' said Flo. 'But analysing the material found under her fingernails should be useful. Forensics also collected every scrap of rubbish and detritus from the area near the body, so we may get lucky.'

I picked at my cuticles in agitation, and George tutted at me.

'Your sister does that too. It must be genetic.'

Before I could comment on some of his irritating habits, Joe re-entered the meeting room, carrying a printout.

'I found Sandor on the database. He married another British woman after divorcing Gladys, a Mary Forrest. They had a daughter, Sophia, who took her mother's maiden name. Mary died of cancer in the 1970s and Sandor has disappeared. We will have to research his present whereabouts.'

'Mouse found Joy for Gladys. Perhaps he came across Sandor during his search. Do you want me to ask him?' I said.

'Andy is busy studying for his degree,' said George. 'I don't want him getting mixed up in police business.'

I winced at George's use of Mouse's real name. Mouse did not like George calling him Andy. It reminded him of his former existence, which included a spot of carjacking and some illegal hacking. He had grown up a lot since moving in with me, but still had occasional tantrums when things didn't go his way.

'Mouse won't be interfering. Gladys asked him to find her adopted daughter who turned out to be Joy. He must have come across Sandor in his trawl through the archives. It's not like we're asking him to do anything other than check his notes.'

'It might save us a ton of time, gov,' said Joe. 'We don't have any leads yet.'

George shook his head.

'Absolutely not. I'd prefer if we tried to find Sandor first. Surely, with police resources, we can do better than a teenage boy?'

I almost told him Mouse had left his teens behind, but George would have been annoyed to be corrected. I kept my powder dry. Joe nodded. George looked triumphant.

'So, that's agreed? We'll use Mouse as a last resort. Did Sophia live around here too?'

Joe rustled his printout.

'Erm, no. She lived in Liverpool.'

'She must have travelled to Seacastle to find Joy,' said Flo.

'Why would anyone follow her to Seacastle and kill her?' I asked.

'Maybe she had an abusive boyfriend who wouldn't take no for an answer?' said George. 'We could be dealing with domestic abuse. We need to investigate her love life.'

'Or could Joy have been responsible? It's not like she lacked the training to polish Sophia off. It would explain why Joy has disappeared too,' said Joe.

'You can't be serious,' I said. 'You're suggesting fratricide?'

'Sororicide,' said Flo. 'The act of killing one's sister. A vanishingly rare occurrence, despite the catfights.'

'I'm surprised it doesn't happen more often,' I said. 'I tried to hit Helen with a hockey stick once.'

'Be that as it may,' said George, his voice strained. 'It's hardly likely to be a political assassination. Joe should go to Liverpool and get Sophia's history. It's far more likely she had a violent boyfriend, and she fled to Seacastle in the vain hope of escaping him.'

'But how did she locate Joy?' said Flo.

'She probably used a search agency. Everyone's doing it these days,' said George.

'My missus watches Long Lost Family. It's a real tearjerker,' said Joe.

'But what about her foreign connections?' I asked.

'What about them?' said George, frowning at me. 'Don't go chasing shadows, Tan. It's none of your business. And anyway, this seems to me to be a straightforward case of abuse gone wrong. Joy is a red herring.'

'Joy'll come back eventually,' said Joe. 'And then we'll find out if she knew about Sophia. Until then, I'll visit Liverpool and do some delving into the life of Miss Forrest.'

Chapter 8

Deep in thought, I walked back along the High Street and almost bumped into Grace who emerged from her shop as I approached.

'What did they say?' she said. 'Who killed Joy?'

I couldn't help smiling. Grace had tremendous faith in the British police because of her experience with them. She also had unreal expectations for the timelines of an investigation.

'Have you got time for a coffee?' I said.

She smiled and spun the sign on her door to read 'closed'. She took the door off the latch and popped the key in her pocket. We walked along, avoiding the jostling teenagers in their school uniforms shopping for their lunch in Greggs and the Co-op. One boy bounced Grace's petite frame sideways. I grabbed her arm to stop her from falling over.

'Those children have no respect,' she said, her hands on her hips. 'In Hong Kong they would step off the pavement to let us through. We had a better life there.'

I didn't counter with the fact that she and Max had had to flee Hong Kong because of his participation in the pro-democracy movement. She liked to be right. When we arrived at Second Home, Ghita and Roz shooed us upstairs and made Grace a jasmine tea. I had another latte, despite feeling wired from my time at the station.

'So?' said Roz. 'Spit it out. What happened?'

The news about Sophia Forrest made everyone despondent.

'Have they told Gladys yet?' said Ghita. 'She needs to know.'

'Poor old Gladys,' said Grace. 'She must be going through the washer.'

'The wringer,' said Roz. 'Not that it matters.'

At least it made us smile, even if we were none the wiser about the circumstances. I imagined Ryan's relief when the body in the morgue didn't belong to Joy, and I realised George would question Ryan about Sophia too. But then I remembered Ryan's odd change of mood on the night the body turned up. At first he had been devastated, but later he seemed almost cheerful and convinced Joy was still alive. I thought it most peculiar, but George and Flo had attributed it to shock. The most likely explanation was that he had spoken to her on the telephone. But why hadn't he said so? I had promised George not to interfere in the case, but that was when we thought the secret services were involved. Surely he wouldn't mind if I had a chat with Ryan? After all, Ryan had confided in me alone about their clandestine activities.

I was still wondering about Ryan when I got home after work and spotted Gladys lurking at her window, her hopeful face making me feel guilty. Had someone blabbed about my meeting at the station? I pointed at her door, and she opened it almost immediately. The house smelled of boiled cabbage and vinegar making me wrinkle my nose. Gladys did not notice my reaction.

'You've got news of Joy?' she asked.

'Not exactly. Can I come in?'

'Of course.'

She led me into her sitting room where she perched on the edge of her armchair as if ready for action. I took a deep breath and told her about Sophia. She became silent and slid back in her chair, trying to take in the news. The sound of the electric clock in her kitchen ticking away the hours penetrated the room. I waited.

'Does Sandor know?' she said.

'The police haven't found him yet.'

'But hasn't Mouse located him?'

'George doesn't want to bring Mouse into the case.'

'But that's ridiculous.'

'We're talking about George,' I said, shrugging. 'He told me not to interfere…'

She frowned. I waited for the penny to drop. Then she grinned at me.

'Oh! I get it. He didn't tell me.'

'Neither did I, if anyone's asking. Do you feel up to a bit of investigating? I know Mouse will be thrilled to help you, but don't tell him I sent you. I don't need George getting his knickers into a twist. After all, I'm only trying to help him.'

I hadn't intended to get more involved. George had all the cards, and Joe Brennan was a skilled detective. If Gladys discovered anything, she promised to go straight to the police. But my best intentions flew out of the window when I received a text from Ryan asking me to come to the Shanty. He had never done this before, and a frisson of excitement coursed through my body. Did he have news about Joy?

I invited Harry for a steak and kidney pie as cover for my mission. He never turned down food, especially any meal which featured a pie. We drove to the car park in my Mini, as I didn't intend to drink more than a glass of cider. Instead of getting out when I switched off the ignition and making a beeline for the pub, Harry turned to me, a quizzical look on his face.

'Are you planning on interfering with George's investigation?' he said.

'How can you ask me that?'

'Because I know you pretty well.'

I swallowed.

'Ryan wants to talk to me.'

'Shouldn't you have told George?'

'George is chasing leads in Liverpool. He thinks Sophia may have been attacked by an ex-boyfriend. The disappearance of Joy may not be related to Sophia's death. It could be a coincidence.'

'I thought you didn't believe in coincidences.'

'I don't, but there's always an exception. Ryan might have heard from Joy.'

'Couldn't he have told you on the phone?'

'He's a spy, Harry. He doesn't talk on unprotected networks.'

Harry laughed.

'I didn't realise I was going out with Mata Hari.'

The grass rippled in the western breeze as we walked along the path from the car park. I couldn't help sneaking a glance at the place where Sophia's body had been found. The grass had been flattened by all the foot traffic, and a dark patch still stained the ground. It made me feel sick, and I looked around for something to distract me. I noticed two large clumps of sea kale growing up against the wall of the Shanty and walked towards them. New foliage had emerged in the spring thaw, making them stand out against the whitewash. One had a stand of red valerian growing behind it. I took out my mobile phone and tried to take a photograph using the zoom function to zero in on the pretty pink flowers. Harry tutted behind me.

'Honestly, they grow everywhere. Why are you taking a photo of them?'

'Because I need a new background photograph for my mobile phone.'

Harry pursed his lips, and I focussed on the flowers. Then I saw it; a woven material strap, almost hidden in the shadows among the stems. I took a plastic bag from the supermarket out of my handbag and put it over my hand.

'Why are you doing that?' said Harry. 'Are you allergic to... Oh.'

I pulled a courier-type handbag out of the valerian plants. It had a row of tassels along the flap. Had it been discarded by a pickpocket after removing the wallet? Then a chill ran up my spine.

'I think this could belong to Sophia Forest,' I said, looking back at the murder site. 'She may have thrown it away in the dark so the attacker couldn't find it.'

I carefully pulled the plastic bag over the handbag so as not to contaminate the evidence. Harry scratched his chin.

'Or could it be Joy's handbag? We'd better ask Ryan.'

'I knew you'd think it was a good idea eventually.'

'Don't be a smart arse. Nobody loves a smart arse.'

'You do.'

Ryan had his back to us as we entered the Shanty. The wind slammed the door shut, and he spun his chair around in an instant, his eyes wide with fright. When he saw us, he relaxed immediately, but not before both of us registered it.

Harry approached the bar and stuck out his hand as if nothing had happened.

'All right?' he said. 'Any news of that errant wife of yours? We were so relieved to hear the body didn't belong to Joy.'

'Me too, but I'm slightly worried about the woman they found outside. She looked exactly like Joy. It freaked me out a little.'

'You're not the only one. The police think they might have identified her. She may be Sophia Forrest from Liverpool.'

'Really? That's great news. I mean to say, at least she had been identified. Maybe they can trace her killer too. Have they told her poor family yet?'

'Well, the thing is. Joy is her family. They are half-sisters, sharing the same father.'

Ryan's jaw dropped, and he struggled to speak. I looked at Harry, but he shook his head. I could almost hear him say wait in my head.

'What a horrible coincidence. I'm not sure where to start. Joy travelled to Budapest looking for her father. She left a note in the bedroom drawer telling me not to worry if she dropped off the radar. I found it when searching for a hairbrush, that's why I thought the body wasn't hers, even when it bore a strong resemblance.'

'Her father? But he might be in England. His name is Sandor Sabyani. Can you tell Joy if she gets in contact?'

'Of course. But she hasn't called since the night of the murder. She may be hiding in case it's related to our work.'

'There's something else. I found this outside,' I said, placing the handbag on the bar, still encased in its plastic covering.

'Take a peep inside. Do you recognise this handbag? It was in the bushes beside the pub. Please don't touch it.'

Ryan glance at it.

'It doesn't belong to Joy, if that's what you're asking. She only owns classic nineteen-fifties leather handbags, mostly croc or lizard. She wouldn't be seen dead with a hippy bag like that one. Could it belong to the murdered woman?'

'It might do. Have you got any medical gloves in the house?'

Ryan grinned.

'What a loaded question. I do as it happens. Are we going to have a quick search before we call George?'

'You read my mind,' I said.

'I'm going to put a pie in the oven,' said Harry.

'Plausible deniability?' said Ryan.

'Extreme hunger.'

After I put on a pair of gloves, I persuaded the zip to open and looked inside the bag. It contained the usual assortment of lipsticks and pens, a wallet, a notebook, a bus pass in the name of Sophia Forrest, and an iPhone. There was no sign she planned to stay at the Shanty. No toothbrush or spare underwear. Just the handbag of someone popping in for a quick drink.

'George thinks she might be the victim of domestic abuse and sought refuge with Joy.'

'But where is her overnight bag? Surely she brought more than a handbag?'

'It doesn't add up for me either. George might find clues in the phone.'

I re-zipped the bag and blew away the powder which had escaped from the gloves. Then I sealed it into the plastic bag again just as Harry emerged from the kitchen.

'Would you like chips with your pie?' he asked.

'Are you cooking me one too?' said Ryan. 'I'm starving.'

Harry disappeared back into the kitchen.

Ryan came out from behind the bar carrying knives and forks and napkins and put them on a table. Then he turned around.

'I have a huge favour to ask of you. Can you travel to Budapest and find Joy? I'd go myself, but…' He gestured at his wheelchair. 'It's not the most disabled-friendly of cities.'

'Of course. You'll need to give me a list of her usual haunts and contacts.'

'You'll go? It's a big ask, but I'm worried about Joy. She's my world.'

'I'd do it for any of my friends.'

'I wouldn't expect you to pay for the trip. My bank account is pretty healthy since they paid me the compensation for my injury.'

'Cash would definitely help, but I need you to convince Harry to go with me.'

'Go with you where?' said Harry, carrying out a tray of steaming food.

'On an adventure,' I said.

'I'd go to the ends of the Earth with you,' said Harry. 'And if it's dangerous, you're not going without me.'

'Excellent. That's settled then,' said Ryan. 'Supper's on me. Oh, you're going to need this.'

He reached into the side pocket of his wheelchair and pulled out a small dark blue booklet, which he handed to me with a wink. I opened it to find a crest like the one in my passport and an identification made out in my name, which claimed I worked for MI6 as a special agent. It had a barcode and a QR code, and for all the world resembled an official document.

'You can't give this to me,' I said. 'Aren't there rules about faking documents?'

Ryan cackled.

'We don't carry ID. I bought this on Etsy. It's for cosplay. Brilliant isn't it?'

Harry took it from me and scrutinised it.

'Uncanny,' he said. 'It looks real.'

'You might need it,' said Ryan. 'I've used one before. People almost faint when you flash them.'

'Thanks. You're a star. I'll keep it safe, just in case,' I said. 'Oh! There is one more thing.'

'You sound more like Columbo every day,' said Harry, rolling his eyes.

'It's important for Ryan to know.'

'Know what?'

'Gladys Fitch is Joy's mother.'

Chapter 9

Ryan was suitably gobsmacked by the news that Joy's mother had been living in Seacastle a few minutes away from the Shanty. He promised not to tell Joy the truth about Gladys, if she came home to Seacastle, but to let Gladys tell Joy herself. He also agreed to keep Gladys updated with the latest news from Budapest. Gladys did not appreciate us telling Ryan about her. She took the news of our trip to Budapest badly too.

'You can't go there without me. It's my daughter who's missing.'

'Be reasonable. We're pretending to go on a dirty weekend together. How many people would bring a pensioner with them?' I asked.

'I could pretend to be your mother.'

Harry laughed.

'I definitely wouldn't take my mother with me if I was planning some hanky-panky.'

I punched his arm to shut him up.

'We can't afford to take you with us and anyway we need you to follow up on Sandor with Mouse. It's vital you find Sandor before he disappears for good.'

'And why would he do that?'

'He's the link between the two sisters. He may be the reason Sophia is dead.'

'Why don't you let George look for him instead and let me come with you? You think I'm too old, don't you?' said Gladys. 'That I'll slow you down.'

'Don't be silly. You're as fit as a fiddle.'

'How old are you?' asked Harry.

'A gentleman never asks a lady her age.'

'I don't think anyone's ever called me that before,' said Harry, winking.

'You're too important,' I said. 'How would Joy cope if something happened to you? She just lost a sibling. I don't want her to lose you before you are reunited.'

That appeared to hit home. Gladys promised to call Mouse and arrange a meetup in Chichester so they could research Sandor's whereabouts.

'And don't forget to keep us informed,' I said. 'You may find Sandor's address for us to visit.'

Her sulky face did not inspire confidence, but we didn't have time to placate her. Ryan had booked us flights on Wizz Air from Gatwick in two days' time and we had packing to do. Harry insisted I buy some digestive biscuits and tea bags to take with us as emergency rations. I popped into Marks and Spencers to get them, and, on a whim, bought a black negligee too. Harry found it lying on top of my carry-on bag.

'And what, may I ask, is this for?' he said, dangling it in the air.

'You're the one who called me Mata Hari. I'm taking this spying lark seriously.'

'Oh, don't worry. If you wear this, I shall play my role with gusto.'

'I should hope so too.'

'Do you want to practise?'

I did. Practice makes perfect.

The Wizz Air flight left Gatwick the next day in the afternoon. We took the train from Seacastle to avoid paying for parking at the airport. We had flexible tickets for the return flight, just in case we needed to stay longer than a week. My stomach filled with butterflies as we waited to board the aeroplane. Who did we think we were? George had a point about leaving it to the experts. I ignored his better instincts.

The flight left on time, and we were lucky to find a small queue at Budapest's airport immigration. After we passed through the frantic ranks of the amateur taxi drivers trying to grab our suitcases and take us to their vehicles, we exited onto the roadway where buses, cars and taxis milled around, pulling in and out from the pavement. We had pre-booked a taxi, and the taxi driver, a small, wiry man with an enormous moustache held up a sign as we came out of the arrivals hall.

'You first visit with Budapest?' he asked, smiling.

I had been to Budapest years ago, but I suspected his vocabulary to be limited, so I nodded and smiled. We followed a railway line for much of the journey into Budapest. I found the drive to the centre of town similar to many ex-Soviet occupied cities in Europe, starting with the outer limits where a mix of nineteen-sixties communist blocks mixed with newer commercial buildings, garages and cargo storage buildings. A large Tesco loomed into view and out again before I could register. As we neared town, small bungalows with tiled roofs sitting on either side of tree-lined roads at right angles to the main road. Two large modern concert halls lurked side by side like giant glass toads. Ash and sycamore trees were ubiquitous and provided shade from the midday sun. Horse chestnuts in bloom provided colour in the parks and playgrounds.

I found it slightly unnerving not to understand a single poster or road sign. Like many British people, I have a smattering of basic French and Spanish, but Hungarian appeared as impenetrable as Chinese to me. I realised I couldn't even greet or thank people in their language, something I was determined to remedy. Ryan had told me Hungarians take manners for granted and they would appreciate polite greetings. I had been learning phonetic pronunciations of common phrases and repeated them to distract Harry, who had been scanning the population on the footpaths.

'I haven't got time to learn Hungarian,' he said. 'We should divide and conquer on this one. You greet people, and I'll kill them.'

Harry's idea of a joke, but I still experienced a shiver down my spine. Harry would not mess around if we encountered trouble. Joy's disappearance had become more real since we had arrived in a strange city where neither of us spoke the language. I crossed my fingers we would come across some English speakers, or worst case, French or Spanish who could help us find her. The taxi got snarled up in traffic once we reached the centre of town. We crawled along the Danube, admiring the beautiful bridges spanning the river.

'Buda here. Other side Pest,' said the driver.

'Seriously?' said Harry.

'That's what it says here,' I replied, shoving my phone at him. 'They used to be separate cities on either side of the River Danube.'

We drove down a series of side streets and passed several cute boutique hotels I would have given an arm or leg to stay in and finally stopped outside a shabby building with a filthy awning which read Grand Hotel Budapest. I didn't appreciate their sense of humour.

Harry paid the taxi from our stash of Hungarian currency given to us by Ryan with no ceremony in a Tesco shopping bag.

'Only change money in the banks if you need more,' he said. 'The street changers will rip you off, and it's illegal.'

The swing door of the hotel had a maze of cracks running through it, surrounding a circular hole. I had the awful feeling it might have been left by a bullet, but I kept my thoughts to myself. The interior hinted at past grandeur with its shabby velvet curtains and ornate cornices, but a slight whiff of disinfectant did not inspire confidence about the state of the rooms. An online booking site had called it full of old-world charm, otherwise known as gloomy, tatty and smelling of mould.

My regret at using the same hotel as Joy intensified with the memory of the lovely hotels we had passed in the taxi. I wondered if there would be Wi-Fi in the rooms and imagined Mouse's reaction if the answer turned out to be no. The hotel would not have met with his approval. The boy had expensive taste. We approached the dark wooden reception desk, and I handed over our passports and the printed reservation for the hotel to the severe young woman behind the desk. She reminded me of Sally Wright on a bad day. She took the passports into an office behind the desk, and I could hear a photocopier whirring. I filled in the registration form for both of us, trying not to feel impatient with the entire process. The receptionist slapped the passports down on the desk, along with a key. I stared at it stupidly before Harry picked it up and thanked her.

'Up the stairs. Fourth floor,' she barked at us.

I almost giggled, although I saved my breath for the stairs. Harry insisted on carrying both bags and staggered up the last flight of stairs puffing and bright red in the face. There was no point in offering to help him. He wouldn't have let me. We both leant on the flock wallpaper, panting outside our room before we let ourselves in. The interior had wonky floorboards, which creaked loudly as we entered. The carpet yelled nineteen eighties, and the furniture wouldn't have looked out of place in my shop. There were two mismatched beds, one of which had a lumpy mattress. I pulled back the covers on the other bed.

'The sheets are clean at least,' I said.

'Joy really knew how to live it up,' said Harry. 'No wonder the hotel was so cheap.'

'Are you hungry?' I asked.

'Starving.'

'Let's sit in a touristy café with menus in English. I don't think I can face fighting my way through one written in Hungarian.'

'Good plan. Have you found one that looks good?'

Five minutes later we were sitting in the 0,75 Bar and Bistro on Saint Stephen's Square. Outside it, small groups of tourists, also out for a bite to eat, were admiring the famous basilica. The menu almost made me drool with anticipation. Finally, I chose duck, and Harry chose goulash.

'What else would I eat in Hungary?' he said. 'Shall we have a nice bottle of red wine?'

'Can we afford it?'

'Ryan told me to treat you to a proper break. You spend your life helping your friends, but you never ask for anything. That's why they love you.' He gazed into my eyes. 'That's why I love you.'

I blushed, thoughts of Joy vanquished for a moment. He stroked my hair, and I leaned into his hand. The waiter arrived with the wine and gave us a knowing smile. I guessed he saw his fair share of courting couples at the restaurant. Harry took a glug of his wine.

'Delicious.' He wiped his mouth with his napkin and leaned forward. 'But why come here now? Joy, I mean. Ryan told us she was looking for her father, but she's had the whole secret service apparatus available for years and she never used it before.'

'The same reason Gladys did, I expect. Time waits for no one. Perhaps they both felt the same longing to assemble the puzzle and form a family.'

He took another mouthful of wine and frowned.

'I suppose so. But what if the truth is more sinister? We might find ourselves completely out of our depth. And where do we start? Budapest is not a small city.'

'I vote we start with the receptionist. If this is Joy's chosen hotel, they must remember her. Could they have seen her with someone? Or has a person come calling for her and left their details? She might have an arrangement with them to keep her messages.'

'All good points. Ah, here comes our food. Can we eat without discussing conspiracy theories, please? I don't want to get an acid stomach.'

We hardly spoke during dinner. The food hit the spot and washed down easily on a river of wine. By the time we headed home, I felt a little tipsy. Harry paid the bill with another wodge of forints and left a generous tip. We walked out of the restaurant into the square and turned back towards the street on which our hotel lay. I glanced back at the square and thought I saw a shadow slip into a doorway. The hairs on my neck stood up.

'Did you see that?' I asked Harry who was whistling cheerfully and gazing up at the buildings.

'See what, sweetheart? I only see you looking radiant in the moonlight.'

'Don't be silly. I'm serious. I think someone's following us.'

Harry stopped dead in his tracks and scanned the street behind us. Nothing moved. We stood stock still for what seemed like forever, but there was no sign of anyone else on our street. Then a cat yowled and bumped among the bins in an alley behind us.

'It was a cat. You are imagining things,' said Harry. 'You're bound to be nervous. I've been in this sort of situation before, so it's different for me.'

I shrugged. 'Perhaps. Let's get back to our hotel. I'm tired.'

But I had seen something. Definitely.

Chapter 10

I woke the next morning with a pounding headache caused by extreme dehydration from the flight and too much red wine. Harry snored happily beside me as I struggled to extract a paracetamol from my handbag. I swallowed it with some bottled water and took my mobile phone off the charger. After visiting TripAdvisor to leave a positive review for 0,75 Bistro, I checked my WhatsApp messages and found one from George marked 'Urgent'. I opened it and skimmed through the contents, alarm rising in my chest. Someone had broken into Second Home over night. I shook Harry away and shoved the screen in his face.

'Where's the fire?' he said, scrabbling on the bedside cabinet for his reading glasses. He read the message, glancing at me with concern as he got the gist. 'You'd better ring him straight away.'

'I can't get Wi-Fi here. Let's go to a café and have coffee and a bun and I'll call George from there.'

The water in the shower was lukewarm at best, so I didn't dawdle in there despite the urge to wash away my hangover. We got dressed and staggered down the three flights of stairs to the lobby. The severe receptionist tutted as I approached her.

'Good morning,' I said, in my ropey Hungarian. 'Please can you direct us to a café?'

I had only learned four or five phrases, despite my constant revision of a ten basic phrases video I found on YouTube. I hoped she would not be scornful of my accent. To my astonishment, a radiant smile crossed her face.

'Ah, you speak Hungarian? I am so happy. The best café is around the corner. Tell them Magda sent you.'

'Koszonom,' I said.

She beamed.

'Jo etvagyat!'

Harry tugged my sleeve as we left the hotel.

'What did she say?'

'I think she said enjoy it, but all the letters run together in Hungarian. It's an impossible language.'

'And you learned on the bus?'

'About five phrases. And I practiced them while you were in the shower.'

'I'm going to buy you breakfast for that piece of spy craft.'

'Excellent. I'm starving.'

When we arrived at the café, I let Harry order using hand gestures and pointing, while I used the Wi-Fi to call George. He answered on the first ring.

'Tan, is that you?'

'What on earth happened?'

'Someone broke into Second Home last night.'

'Did they take anything?'

'I'm not sure. Your shop is full of bric-a-brac. How am I supposed to know what's missing?'

'Is Roz there?'

'Yes, she's been checking the stock. She isn't sure either. She told me to tell you not to worry. They took nothing from the counter cabinet. I'm pretty sure someone broke in by mistake, thinking there might be valuable antiques inside.'

'They'll have been disappointed then,' I said, laughing.

'We've got the perpetrator on CCTV, I hope. Rohan and Kieron have a camera at the outside door of Surfusion, which records the activity on the street. Luckily it was working last night, so I'll soon find out who perpetrated this. I'll get the handyman to fix the lock for you and give Roz the new key.'

'Thanks George. I really appreciate it.'

'What are you doing in Budapest, as if I couldn't guess?'

'Harry and I are having a romantic getaway.'

'Romantic, my arse. Don't get into trouble over there. I can't help you out if something goes wrong.'

'We'll be careful. I'm hoping Joy turns up while we are still playing detective out here.'

George harrumphed.

'You're Harry's problem now, anyway. I'll get that door fixed.'

He hung up before I could protest. I put away my phone and Harry and I sat outside at a pavement table enjoying the morning sunshine.

'What did George say?' said Harry. 'Did the burglar steal anything valuable?'

'Apparently not. They may have been disturbed because they didn't even take the trinkets from the display cabinet.'

'Now, that's odd. Were they targeting specific items?'

'Honestly? There's nothing worth stealing in Second Home, except for the icon, but that's in the pub with Ryan.'

'Should we let him know?'

'I expect he'll call me today with news of one sort or another. Let's wait and see what he says.'

After we finished a leisurely breakfast, we walked back to the hotel to top up our phone charges and collect our day packs. I had eaten far too much and groaned as I entered the lobby. The receptionist smiled as she saw us enter.

'You enjoyed your breakfast?' she asked.

'Yes, thank you,' said Harry. 'It was finom.'

'You speak Hungarian too?'

'Not really. We can only say a few words.'

'Most tourists can't say thank you or good morning,' she said. 'It is not polite. You are different.'

I saw my chance to ask some questions.

'Does Joy Wells speak Hungarian well?'

She froze like a rabbit in the headlights. I tried again.

'We have a friend who stays in this hotel. Her name is Joy Wells. Do you know her?'

She shook her head vigorously.

'I'm sorry, I haven't met anyone with that name.'

But I noticed her head bobbing as if to negate that statement. She had lied to me. Her eyes darted back and forth in panic, trying to avoid my searching gaze. I decided not to push her. Harry smiled at her.

'Are you sure?' he said. 'We can show you a photograph if that helps.'

I thought she might run away. She resembled a startled deer. Then she pulled herself together.

'Of course I am sure,' she said, as her face reverted to its severe mask. 'You can't expect me to remember every tourist that stays a night at this hotel.'

I could see him about to probe her about her answer, but I pulled his sleeve and made him follow me upstairs.

'She lied to you,' said Harry, puffing as we headed to our room. 'She definitely remembers who Joy is.'

'Perhaps she knows something about Joy's disappearance. She looked scared.'

'We'll need to ask her again later.'

'If she'll talk to us. I wonder why she looked so frightened.'

We lay on the bed, our stomachs distended from our enormous breakfast.

'What's our next move?' I asked.

'You're the sleuth.'

I didn't answer. I felt a little foolish rushing over to Budapest without a plan. It wasn't as if I could ask for help from the local police. Going to the British embassy would not be the best plan, either. My mobile phone vibrated in my hand, and I answered it.

'Hi, it's Ryan.'

I sat up in bed and put my pillow behind my back.

'Ryan? Have you heard from Joy?'

'No. I haven't. But I have searched all her papers, and I've found a few names and addresses from Budapest she wrote in a notebook. I recognise one name, a man called Imre Szabo. He owns a bookshop in the Jewish quarter. Joy trusted him.'

'That's fantastic. Can you text me the information?'

'I'm sending you everything I've got.'

'Did you hear about the robbery at my shop?'

'No. I'm so sorry. Perhaps someone discovered you would be away. Did they steal anything?'

'Nothing of value. Is the icon stored safely?'

'It's in my sock drawer, but I'll put it in the safe now. Thanks for the heads up.'

'It may be worthless, but who knows?'

'Do you think someone wanted the icon?'

'I hadn't considered it. I can't imagine the only person who showed an interest in the icon tried to burgle the shop.'

'It may have been drug addicts. They only take cash for their next fix.'

'They'd be out of luck in my shop. We leave no cash in the till.'

'I'll send you those addresses. Good luck and enjoy Budapest. It's a wonderful city.'

'Thank you. It's certainly beautiful and steeped in secrets. If Joy's here somewhere, we'll find her.'

Ryan hung up, and I put the top of the phone to my lips as I pondered what he had said.

'Ryan?' said Harry.

'Yes. He's texting us some useful addresses.'

Five minutes later, my mobile pinged loud in the high-ceilinged room.

'Is that the list?'

'Yes. How interesting! One of Joy's contacts, Gretchen Horvath, runs a restaurant at the Memento Park outside Budapest. I read about it on Google before we came to Budapest. They say it's amazing, like a graveyard of Communist art. We could take a cab there, if you fancy. Joy also has a friend in the Jewish Quarter nearby who owns a bookshop. We can pay him a visit tomorrow morning.'

'I'd rather go to the bookshop.'

'Don't be a wet blanket. It's a lovely sunny day and it might rain tomorrow. You can think of it as exercise.'

Chapter 11

We hailed a taxi. I felt around for my seatbelt but realised the driver had tucked them under the back seat. I'm not keen on driving anywhere without a seatbelt on, but I assumed the law was different in Hungary. The driver gunned the engine of the ancient taxi and hurtled out of town with no regard for the other drivers or pedestrians. All thoughts of admiring the scenery disappeared as I shut my eyes for most of the journey. When I opened them, I could see Harry's white jaw muscles almost vibrating with stress. Finally, he cracked.

'Too fast,' he said. 'Slow down.'

'Not speaking English,' said the driver.

'Slow down. No hurry.'

'No hurry. Oh, I hurry.'

Harry rolled his eyes at me. Luckily, we screeched to a halt outside the restaurant with no pieces falling off. I tumbled out of the car, almost being sick on the pavement from relief. Harry paid the driver and I could see the stress leave his shoulders as the taxi drove away.

'Bloody lunatic,' he said. 'Are you okay?'

'A little seasick, but I'll get over it.'

The interior of the restaurant was dark. I checked the opening hours written on the door.

'We've got two hours to wait. Do you feel like visiting the Memento Park? It's supposed to be full of statues from the time of the communist era, like a socialist Disneyland.'

'I can't imagine anything worse, but it's better than nothing.'

His disdain lasted about three minutes. The first thing to greet us as we walked through the gates was an original, sky-blue Trabant car. Harry crooned with delight and made me take a photograph of him at the wheel. I tapped the bonnet and was astounded to find it was made of plastic fibre of some sort. The wind-up windows still functioned too.

'This car used to be the fantasy of most families in the Soviet Union, you know.'

'It's not much older than the taxi we came in.'

'Probably safer.'

We made our way through the park, stopping to marvel at the gigantic statues of Marx, Lenin, Engels and other figures from the era. Allegorical monuments featuring personalities from the labour movement and soldiers of the Soviet Red Army towered over us as we walked past them. I found them disturbing and wonderful in equal measure. Harry seemed transfixed by one particular tableau of soldiers headed off to war called the Bela Kun Memorial. I didn't mock him for his previous comments. I hadn't expected to be captivated, either.

'Extraordinary,' he muttered.

We visited the annex where we watched a film on spy craft. It made me wonder if Joy had come across spies using similar methods. An enormous pair of plaster boots occupied the centre of the exhibition, which featured vignettes detailing the days of the nineteen fifty-six revolution. They were replicated outside in bronze on a tall plinth. They are a copy of Stalin's boots, which remained on the pedestal at parade Square after a crowd revolting against communist oppression sawed Stalin's statue off at the knees. I muttered the words to Ozymandias under my breath.

Two hours flew by before we made our way to the restaurant. Light flooded out of the open door. A delicious smell of cooking wafted out to greet us and my mouth salivated.

'Let's eat here,' I said. 'It smells divine.'

'Brilliant plan.'

A woman with a bun of black hair streaked with silver came over to us, wiping her hands on an apron.

'You are welcome. Do you wish to eat? It's rather early for dinner.'

'Actually, it's late for lunch,' I said. 'How did you know we were English?'

'Just a guess. Did you go to the park?'

'Yes, we did. It's unusual. I wasn't sure what I thought about it.'

'It's a reminder of recent history for the older generation. The collapse of communism in nineteen-ninety led to the removal of all these monuments. Some people wanted to destroy them and melt them down, but the Municipality established this park instead. The younger generation just makes Tiktoks here. They were born after the fall of communism and don't understand how we suffered.'

'We remember it well,' said Harry. 'As a matter of fact, we were hoping to connect with a friend of ours in Budapest, who spent the end of the Cold War here.'

I saw her stiffen and reach out for the counter.

'Really? Have you found him?'

'She's a woman,' I said. 'Joy Wells. Her husband told us you are friends. I hoped she might have visited you recently.'

She backed away from him and I wondered if his army bearing had frightened her. He had military written all over him, from the shaved head to the barrel chest.

'I don't remember anyone of that name.'

'Are you sure? Her husband found your name in her address book. Isn't it Gretchen Horvath?'

'You are mistaken. My name is Maya Toren.'

'Oh. I'm sorry. We thought you were the owner.'

'I am. There's no Gretchen Horvath here. I'd like you to leave, please.'

'But we were hoping to eat,' said Harry.

'I don't serve food before seven.'

My stomach growled at me in protest as she showed us the door. I couldn't believe she threw us out.

'Did Ryan get it wrong?' said Harry.

'Didn't you see the initials on her apron? GH as plain as day.'

'What's she so scared of?'

'I have no idea, but it may explain Joy's disappearance.'

'Didn't she come here to search for her family?'

'That may have been the initial reason, but with Sophia's death perhaps things have become more complicated. What if someone killed her thinking she was Joy, and that same person is now hunting Joy in Budapest?'

'Perhaps Joy warned her contacts not to talk to anyone?' said Harry.

'That would explain her over-reaction to our question. What do we do now?'

'I'm so hungry I could eat my own arm. Let's get a taxi back to town and eat near the hotel.'

'Can we take a slower taxi?'

'We can try.'

I looked around to see if I could spot a taxi rank. The only car belonged to a middle-aged man with an old-fashioned Irish tweed cap pulled down over his face as if he was asleep.

'I don't suppose he wants to take us into town,' I said.

'Come on. Let's walk to the junction. We'll pick up one there.'

Soon we were heading back into town, in a newer and slower vehicle. We stopped at the same café where we had eaten breakfast and had a local stew with fresh bread and a few beers.

'That didn't advance our search much,' said Harry. 'What's our next move?'

'We should visit Joy's friend in the Jewish Quarter who owns a bookshop. We can pay him a visit tomorrow morning.'

'Let's hope he's more forthcoming than Mrs Kovacs.'

'Perhaps she's suspicious of us and protecting Joy. This spying lark may be more complicated than we think.'

Chapter 12

Szabo Books lurked on a side street in the old Jewish Quarter of Budapest near the Great Synagogue. Google informed me that the bookstore contained literature in the English language. This made me hopeful Imre Szabo would speak English. Two stone archways with inner wooden frames painted a faded teal formed the front of the bookshop. The uppermost part of the archways contained stained glass, and the right-hand arch hosted a double door with glass in the top half. Inside, a counter with a large coffee machine and a display cabinet with tasty treats occupied the centre of the small front room. I peered through into the cluttered interior with its black and white tiled linoleum floor covered in cigarette burns. Not only were books lined up in double file on the shelves, but stacks of books occupied every nook and cranny of the shop. Harry pushed the door open for me to enter. I realised the bookshop continued far into the building and out of a back window I could see a shady nook with tables and chairs in a garden filled with trees. The heady smell of old paper filled my sinuses and reminded me of my old school library.

'Why do books smell so booky?' asked Harry, rubbing his nose.

'Books are made from trees. Their signature smell comes from the lignin rotting in their pages,' said a man who stepped out of the shadows.

He was about seventy years old. He had a bald head with tufts of grey hair sticking out over his ears. His pockmarked face had heavy black brows and more hairs emerging from his nostrils. He had a slight hump on his back, so he looked up at us from his bowed head. His gnarled hand wavered in front of us.

'Imre Szabo at your service,' he said, looking us up and down. 'You're not here to buy books are you?'

'Not primarily,' I said.

'We understand you know a woman called Joy Wells. Only, she's a friend of ours and she's gone missing. Her husband is worried about her,' said Harry.

'Joy? I haven't seen her for weeks,' he said. 'Would you like a cup of coffee?'

'Yes please,' I said.

He stood beside the coffee machine and loaded it up with ground coffee. The sounds of spoons on crockery and the whistle of the steamer filled the shop. I scanned the shelves of the shop, hoping to find something I could buy. I spotted a travel section and read the spines in the second-hand section. I pulled out the Lonely Planet's Pocket guide to Budapest, a perfect size to carry in my bag. I flipped through it and found the useful phrases section. I needed to keep refreshing my memory so I could tackle Magda later on without Harry. Imre loaded a tray containing a pot of coffee, a sugar bowl and three cups with spoons in them.

'Come through to the back,' he said. 'It's more private.'

We walked through a narrow room with coffee tables and chairs to one side and books lining the walls and entered another with multi-paned windows looking over a sunny grass square. We sat at a round table half covered in books. I could feel grains of sugar under my hands as I leaned on the table when I sat down. Imre had made the coffee in chipped stoneware mugs and added sugar without asking us. I sipped mine. It was strong enough to trot a mouse across the top. I tried not to grimace. Imre studied our faces.

'So, who am I dealing with?'

'I'm Tanya Bowe.'

'Ah, the private detective. Joy told me all about your talents. And you?'

'I'm Harry Fletcher.'

'Ex-military, am I right? I can always tell.'

'That's right,' said Harry. 'It's a pleasure to meet you.'

'Joy has told me about you. She and I have a long history together you know. She is an exceptionally brave and resourceful woman. We worked together throughout the Cold War. She took enormous risks for her sources. Her husband, Ryan, who was as foolhardy as her, got shot rescuing an agent.'

'Do you still work together?' I asked.

He took a gulp of coffee and took his time placing it back onto the table.

'Sometimes.'

'We believe she might have come to Budapest trying to trace her family,' I said.

He rubbed his chin with his hand.

'Here? Why would she be searching here? I thought she was the most English of English women. So proper, so educated.'

'Her grandparents were Hungarian Jews. They sent her mother, Miriam, to England before they disappeared, where she was brought up as Gladys Finch.'

'So why is Joy searching here?'

'She doesn't know about Gladys yet, but her father was Hungarian too, a man called Sandor Sabyani.'

'How extraordinary. She never told me that.'

'She probably wasn't aware. Her mother gave her up for adoption when she was under a year old,' I said.

'And how do you know that?'

'Because she lives next door to me. She's eighty something now and she traced Joy through the British adoption agency.'

'Truth is stranger than fiction. Why do I bother selling all these novels? So, Joy is searching for her mother, and her mother is searching for her. What about her father?'

'We haven't been able to find him either, but his family came from Budapest too. Is there anywhere we can find information about Gladys's parents?'

'The Hungarian Jewish Archive has compiled a complete history of the Jewish population of Hungary. It's close by if you want to visit.'

'Would Joy have gone there?'

'It's highly likely. I can't think why she didn't ask me for help, though.'

He scratched his head.

'Does Joy have any enemies in Budapest?' said Harry.

'You mean like spies with a grudge?' said Imre with a twinkle in his eye. 'The Cold War is over, Mr Fletcher.'

Harry pursed his lips. I thought it was time we left.

'Can you give us the address of the archive please?' I asked.

'Of course. Give me a minute.'

He hobbled across to his desk and wrote it on a piece of paper. Harry stood outside watching some boys playing football in the street. I could tell he was miffed at Szabo's joke. I joined Imre at the counter and offered to pay for the book.

'Oh, take it. The tram company gives me all the copies that get left by tourists. This book will return too.'

'Thank you.'

'And tell me if you find Joy. I'll keep my feelers out here and inform you if I hear anything. Where can I find you?'

'The Grand Hotel, where Joy normally stays.'

'That ghastly dive? Oh well, I guess it makes sense. They must be aware of her comings and goings there. Have you spoken to the staff yet?'

'Not successfully.'

'They must remember something. Ask again.'

'We will. Thank you.'

'Bloody cheek,' said Harry, as I came out. 'I'm no schoolboy.'

'He was joking,' I said. 'Let's go.'

'Do you want to walk?'

'Sure, it looks close by here.'

As we headed down the street, I noticed a woman in a grey coat and a large floppy hat at the corner of the street. She seemed familiar somehow, but I couldn't place her. It definitely wasn't Joy, but then I recognised her.

'Gladys?'

'Where?' said Harry.

'There on the corner. Oh, she's gone.'

'Are you sure?'

'Positive. I told you someone followed us the other night. Come on.'

We set off trotting and rounded the corner. There was no sign of Gladys, but I wasn't deterred.

'I don't see her,' said Harry.

'Wait. You monitor that side and I'll do this side.'

We stood still for several minutes. Harry's patience waned, and he shifted his weight from foot to foot. Then I saw it. A flash of grey behind a large shrub down the road from me. The hem of a coat. I took off again with a surprised Harry several yards behind me. When I checked the bush, a shame-faced Gladys stepped out from behind it.

'Gladys. What on earth are you doing here?'

She shrugged.

'I couldn't stay at home and wonder. I just couldn't.'

Harry shook his head.

'What if Joy returns to the Shanty?'

'Ryan can look after her there. She's my daughter and I'm worried about her. You'd go looking if Mouse was missing, wouldn't you?'

She had a point.

'Well, you're here now. Will you come to the Jewish archives with us? We may dig up some information about your parents.'

'It won't be good news,' said Harry. 'Are you prepared for the truth?'

'Is anyone?' said Gladys. 'But I can't bear the not-knowing anymore.'

'Fair enough. According to the bloke in the bookshop, it's just up the road.'

Chapter 13

The Family Research Centre sat behind the Grand Synagogue in a stone-faced building with twelve reliefs on the facade symbolising the twelve tribes of Israel with the names of the tribes in Hebrew. We were buzzed into a shabby lobby with a lift and some stone stairs and proceeded upstairs to the Gyokerek centre where the databases and resources for family research were stored.. We followed the signs to enquiries and entered a room with forest green faux-leather tub chairs. The chrome and glass counter seemed odd in this staid building. Plastic holders on the glass contained leaflets in nearly every European language.

'Mouse would be furious,' said Gladys, sifting through them. 'He says we shouldn't use paper anymore.'

'Most people who visit us can't operate a computer,' said a tall, elegant woman who appeared from behind a partition. 'Many of them are almost blind, partially deaf and unable to walk further than the bathroom. I'm Katalin, by the way. And you are?'

'I'm Tanya. This is Harry.'

'And this young lady?'

'Gladys Fitch, but my real name is Miriam Steinberg. My parents lived in Budapest during the Second World War.'

'Did they escape before the Nazis arrived?'

'I'm not sure. That's why I'm here. My parents sent me to England in the early days of the war, intending to follow me there. When I arrived, I was placed with a couple for fostering. But my parents never came to get me, so I was adopted by the English couple, the Fitches.'

'Are you aware of the history of the Jewish people in Budapest?'

'No, but I'd be interested in hearing it.'

'Please make yourselves comfortable.'

I sat in a tub seat made hot by the morning sun. I dreaded hearing the truth. Gladys had turned as pale as paper. Harry sat between us and took our hands in his warm, calloused ones. I glanced gratefully at him and noticed he had closed his eyes. Katalin took in a deep breath before starting an awful story she must have told a thousand times. Her face bore the marks of suffering, and I wondered if she was as old as she looked or just worn down by her sadness and the grief of others.

'Before World War II, about two-hundred-thousand Jews lived in Budapest. These numbers were swelled by thirteen-thousand refugees from the rest of Europe before and during the war. Budapest acted as a haven for Jews until the Nazis occupied Hungary in March nineteen-forty-four.'

'What happened then?' said Gladys.

'That's when the authorities ordered the Jews to leave their houses and move into buildings marked with the Star of David. Then, approximately twenty-five thousand Jews were rounded up from the suburbs and transported to the Auschwitz-Birkenau camp. In

November of nineteen-forty-four, seventy-thousand Jews were marched to camps in Austria from where they were sent to various concentration camps, although some were used as slave labour in the construction of fortifications around the city of Vienna. The remaining Jews in Budapest were moved to a ghetto by early December. Between then and the end of January nineteen-forty-five as many as twenty-thousand Jews were taken out of the ghetto and shot along the banks of the Danube. When Soviet forces liberated Budapest in February of the same year, only about one hundred thousand Jews remained alive.'

'Less than half the population?' said Harry. 'What barbarity.'

'No wonder my parents didn't come to England,' said Gladys. 'When I was little, Mabel Fitch told me my actual parents didn't come to get me because they didn't want me anymore. She never said they were from Hungary, or that they were Jewish. I guess she didn't want to answer my questions.'

'Couldn't or wouldn't?' I said. 'She sounds like a nasty woman.'

'That's not fair,' said Gladys. 'They did their best. They didn't want me getting ideas and going to look for them. I would have ended up behind the Iron Curtain.'

'Would you like me to search the archives for you?' said Katalin. 'If you come back tomorrow afternoon, I can also check the vault for any belongings left by your parents.'

Gladys choked.

'Belongings?'

'It's not impossible. I can definitely trace them in the city records. I may discover what happened to the

Steinbergs, but often there is no record. You must be prepared for bad news.'

'I need to uncover the truth so I can be at peace with myself.'

'Okay then. I'll see you here tomorrow. You might be lucky, although it's strange to think that finding out how your parents were murdered counts as any sort of luck at all.'

We left the building and were hit by blazing sunlight which bleached the street and made us screw up our eyes. We walked past a small fenced off area containing stones with names and dates inscribed on them. When I looked it up in my guidebook, I found out the Dohany Street graveyard was used to bury the Jews who died in the ghetto. This deviated from Jewish tradition as burial on synagogue grounds is normally a forbidden practice. Beside the graveyard, a memorial known as the tree of life shimmered silver in the sunlight like a metallic willow. The plaque outside stated that the metal leaves were engraved with the names of Holocaust victims. The horror had not diminished despite the passing of almost a century.

'Where are you staying?' I asked Gladys.

She shrugged.

'Nowhere yet. I hid my bag in the park across from your hotel. My credit card doesn't work here.'

'You slept on a bench?' said Harry.

'I didn't get much sleep to tell you the truth.'

'You might have been attacked, you silly old boot. Why didn't you ask us for help?'

'I thought you'd be angry,' she said, sniffing. 'And I wasn't wrong.'

'Oh, for heaven's sake! I'm not angry with you. Where have you put your bag?'

'I hid it in some bushes.'

'We're going straight there to get it, and then we're booking you into our hotel. It's basic, but it's Joy's preferred hotel in town, so she might turn up there.'

Luckily, nobody had taken a fancy to Gladys's carry-on bag, so Harry pulled it down the street to the hotel. Gladys and I staggered up to our room, resting on the landings, while Harry booked another for Gladys. He appeared after a few minutes and gave us the thumbs up sign.

'They say check-in isn't until three-thirty, so I left Gladys's bag behind the counter. Why don't we rest a minute and then go for lunch nearby?'

Gladys and I lay on the bed while Harry scrolled through his and my phones, reading any pertinent messages out loud.

'I'm sorry,' said Gladys. 'I had to come.'

I patted her hand.

'No, I'm sorry. I had no idea what we would find, but I should have invited you.'

'Mouse sent us a message asking how we are getting on.'

'Tell him I'll call him later. Is he coming home for Easter?' I asked.

'He may want to hang out with his friends at university,' said Harry. 'I would have at that age.'

'What about his pal, Goose?'

'Goose has a year-old baby with another child on the way.'

'He can hang out with us instead,' I said. 'And Hades.'

'He won't be able to resist that offer,' said Harry.

'There's no need to be sarcastic. Mouse loves us.'

'He does,' said Gladys. 'He told me.'

'See? He does,' I said.

'Let's find some lunch. I fancy a goulash.'

Chapter 14

We ate at a local bistro close to our hotel and shared a bottle of wine. Gladys spoke little. The morning's revelations weighed heavily on her and she struggled not to cry, twisting her napkin in her hands. The wine cheered her up a little, but she ate her lunch with the enthusiasm of a convict taking on his last meal. Even Harry's corny jokes could not raise a smile. I wondered how much, if anything, Katalin could discover. I could only imagine Gladys's devastation, if her parents had disappeared into the fog of war without a trace.

We paid for lunch and made our way back to the hotel. Gladys approached the desk to collect the key for her room, which was on the second floor two floors under ours. Magda, the receptionist, had her back to us when we entered and turned to greet us with a smile. When she focused on Gladys, her smile faded, and she stared in disbelief. Gladys, who struggled to pull out the handle of her carry-on bag, did not notice Magda's reaction.

'Can I have the key to my room, please?' she said, without looking up.

Magda recovered her poise almost as quickly as she had lost it.

'Of course, madam. Here you are. Will you need help with your bag?'

'No, thank you. This young man has already offered to carry it upstairs for me.'

Harry grinned and saluted Gladys. I realised I was the only one who picked up on Magda's reaction to Gladys. But what did it mean? My feet ached from walking miles in my pixie boots, and I really fancied a siesta, so I decided to question her later. The sun blazed through the window of our room, so I drew the moth-eaten velvet curtain slightly to cut out the rays and leave us in the turgid air. Harry fell asleep immediately, a legacy of his time in the military when sleep was at a premium. I lay on my side watching the magpies dart past the gap in the curtains, catching the fat flies bumbling between the sprigs of blossom. As I grew drowsy, I tried to clear my mind of the morning's visit so I would not dream of being trapped within a ghetto's walls.

Just as I was dropping off, George rang my mobile phone.

'Tan, is everything all right over there? Gladys has disappeared and Mouse is worried it might be linked to the other incidents.'

'You don't need to worry about Gladys. She followed us to Budapest. She's staying in the room below us.'

'That wicked old woman! I should have known she wouldn't follow orders. Are you making any progress?'

'We have found no clues to the whereabouts of Joy, but we are gathering background on Gladys's family, in case there are any loose ends.'

'I don't think that's a good use of your time. It's ancient history.'

'Has Joe come back from Liverpool?'

'Yesterday.'

'And?'

'And what? It's police business.'

'Don't be like that. He wouldn't have known about Sophia without me.'

George coughed.

'He hit a dead end there. She moved out of her flat about two months ago. We're trying to find out where she moved to next.'

'Did you unlock her phone yet?'

'No. I expect that will give us some useful leads. Thanks for handing in the handbag. I gave the SOCOs a rocket for missing it.'

'But how did she find Joy?'

'We're uncertain. Unless Sandor told her she had a sister? We're still searching for him.'

'He may be dead.'

'Yes, but he could also have moved back to Hungary.'

'I asked the archivist at the Jewish Centre to trace his roots. Maybe they can check if he returned.'

'We don't seem to be getting anywhere in either country. Good luck finding Joy. I'll tell you if we get any leads for you to follow over there.'

'Thanks. I promise to do the same.'

As I hung up, a soft knocking broke the silence. I crept over the creaky floorboards, cringing as I stepped on the crispy corpse of a fly.

'I'll be right there,' I said, leaning over to the peephole.

Magda stood on the landing, looking shifty. I opened the door.

'Is it important? My partner is asleep.'

'I lied to you. Joy Wells is a frequent guest at our hotel. Can you come downstairs to my office? We can speak there in confidence.'

I put my slippers on and followed her downstairs. I debated waking Gladys, but I decided she needed to recover from her traumatic morning and sleepless night. We slipped behind the counter and into a bright office. I screwed up my eyes, having expected it to be as gloomy as the lobby.

'Ah, too much light?' she asked. 'I can close the shutters.'

'No thank you,' I said.

'Please sit here,' she said, patting an old leather couch.

She sat down beside me and put her hands on her knees.

'I don't want you to misunderstand my motives for lying to you. Joy gave me strict instructions to deny ever having met her. It was both for her safety and for mine. Her work can be dangerous, you know. Mostly it's boring. Fact checking, liaison and so on, but it varies.'

'Why have you decided to trust me now?'

She smiled. 'I doubt someone who is obviously a relative of Joy would have lunch with you if you didn't know Joy.'

'What do you mean?'

'Gladys resembles Joy so closely that I assumed they were related.'

'Actually, Gladys is Joy's mother.'

Magda's mouth fell open.

'Her mother? But I thought Joy was adopted.'

'That's right. But Gladys is her birth mother and has searched for her for years. She had to give her up as a baby, because of social mores then. She only found out recently that Joy is her daughter.'

'Oh my goodness, that's amazing!'

'That's why we're here. Joy should have returned to England last week, and her husband is worried sick about her. I couldn't stop Gladys from coming when she knew Joy went missing.'

'Joy didn't stay here long this time,' said Magda. 'She told me someone had been murdered outside her home, someone who looked like her. She was worried they'd come looking for her here in Budapest.'

'But who would want to kill Joy?'

Magda snorted.

'Joy is not short of enemies. Resentments grow bigger over the years, not smaller. She cheated death several times as a younger woman, and not everyone who tried has retired to their dacha yet.'

The hairs on my arms stood up. I had never heard murder discussed so casually, as if it was part of the job, which of course it was in those dangerous days. No wonder Ryan was frantic. Being in a wheelchair must cause him extra frustration. He navigated the pub, and most of Seacastle, with no bother, but Budapest, with its countless steps and high pavements was not exactly wheelchair friendly.

'She's an amazing person. I don't know how she does it.'

'Neither do I.'

'Do you have any idea where she might hide?'

'No. She never gave me any details that might endanger me, or her. I received this letter for her, but she hasn't been back to collect it.' Magda passed me an envelope which had been sitting on the coffee table. 'She told me to give anything which arrived to Ryan, if he came looking for her, but I guess he sent the back-up troops.'

'I'll give this to Gladys. Thank you.'

'I hope you find Joy. She's a brave, intelligent woman. Someone out there wants to harm her.'

'When did you see her last?'

'About a week ago. She packed her bag and left for the airport, but she texted me to say she might be back as her flight was delayed and she hadn't checked in yet. While waiting at the airport, she got a message from Ryan about the murder back home. She returned to the hotel and then disappeared during the night. She didn't tell me where she was headed next.'

I made my way back upstairs and knocked softly on Gladys's door. A groggy voice invited me in. Gladys blinked at me through the bright sunlight.

'Tanya? I was asleep. I dreamed of Joy. What's up?'

'Someone left this envelope in reception for her. Magda thought you should have it.'

'Magda? Oh, the lady at reception.'

'She guessed who you were. Now that I see you again, I must admit, Joy bears a strong resemblance to you. I'm not sure why we didn't notice before. I suppose we weren't looking.'

Gladys took the thin envelope and slid her finger under the flap. She squeaked as the sharp edge nicked it. A drop of blood fell on the contents. A photograph. Sucking her finger, she took it out and peered at it.

'It's a little blurred. Could they be twins?'

She pointed at the photograph. In it, a man in braces held two babies, one in each arm. He was smiling, but he appeared to be thin and tired. I didn't recognise him.

'I suppose so. Does this mean anything to you?'

'No. I don't recognise the man or the children. I've no idea what it signifies.'

'Keep it safe. If someone sent it to Joy, it's important.'

I climbed the stairs to our room and stood in the gap between the curtains, gazing out at the city. Joy was there somewhere. We needed to find her before the murderer did.

Chapter 15

The next morning, Harry and I breakfasted late and took a beautiful walk along the Danube, doing a loop across the river to the Buda district over the Szechenyi chain bridge and back via the Erzsébet bridge. Gladys claimed to be suffering from a migraine and refused to come with us. We left her lying on her bed with a cold compress on her head. She would get rid of it as soon as we left. I didn't mind. I realised she needed to gather her strength for the afternoon's revelations.

As I walked beside Harry, I mused on my relationship with my parents. They may not have been perfect, and they were stuck in the past to an irritating degree, but their constant presence gave me a firm foundation. The Fitches didn't sound like loving parents to me. They saw their adopted daughter as part of a quid pro quo. They brought her up on condition she acted as their unpaid carer when they grew old. Gladys had mentioned a legacy from them. I wondered if there was any more information about the visa payment smuggled out by the Cooks. I could not ask her now, but I make a note to myself to broach the subject when her anxiety lessened.

The city was bathed in spring sunlight, but a bank of black clouds threatened to sweep over the city and drop their cargo, like the threat of invasion. The raw suffering of the Jewish population of Budapest had never struck me before, as I had swallowed the fiction of the city being a haven for them during World War II. I felt privileged to be alive when thousands of people had disappeared for ever. The random nature of their selection worried me when I thought of Gladys's parents. I dreaded going back to the museum to hear what Katalin had discovered. Harry noticed me fretting and squeezed my hand to reassure me. I forced out a smile.

We climbed up Castle Hill in a funicular railway, which we caught at the western end of the chain bridge and rose to the Royal Palace. We did not explore the museums, but we roamed the cobbled alleys with their colourful buildings before heading along the limestone ridge to the gothic Matthias Church and the Fisherman's Bastion with its neo-Romanesque lookout towers. I wished I could take a proper guided tour of the district, but Budapest would still wait for me next time, and Gladys might not.

We descended to the Erzsébet bridge and walked back to our hotel. Gladys waited for us in the lobby, looking older and diminished with sadness. We returned to the museum and upstairs to the department of enquiries. Gladys shuffled with shoulders hunched almost to her ears, like a tortoise sheltering from danger. Katalin greeted us with a practiced smile. I couldn't tell from her expression if she had found anything significant. I noticed Gladys shiver as if someone had walked over her grave. It occurred to me just how traumatic the entire experience was for her. I put an arm around her shoulders, but she didn't acknowledge me. Katalin emerged from behind the counter holding an iPad.

'Good morning. Nice to see you again. Shall we sit down?'

We occupied the same tub seats as before, and Gladys leaned forward with anticipation. Katalin scrolled through her iPad.

'Okay, I'm going to tell you what I've discovered and then we'll move on to the artifacts.'

'Artifacts?' said Gladys, hope or panic in her voice. I couldn't tell.

'Um, belongings, photographs, that sort of thing.'

'Oh, please go on,' said Gladys.

'Your parents, the Steinbergs, moved to Budapest from Sarospatak in nineteen-thirty-six. Your father, Jozsef, was a joiner by trade, and Erzsébet had basic accounting skills. They opened a successful furniture business and made enough money to move to a bigger house in the Jewish quarter of town. When an influx of Jewish refugees arrived in Budapest in the late nineteen-thirties fleeing persecution from the Nazis, Erzsébet became concerned for the family's safety. One of Erzsébet's cousins lived in Austria and she had made friends with Viorica Ursuleac the opera singer. Viorica told her about a pair of English sisters—'

'The Cooks?' said Gladys.

'Exactly. How did you know?'

'I used a young man who's rather good with computers to research my birth mother,' said Gladys.

'We could use someone like him at the archives.'

'I'm afraid he's taken,' I said.

'Anyway, once Gladys had been spirited away to England, the couple prepared their escape. But then the Nazis conscripted Jozsef into the labour service and confiscated their house. Erzsébet had to move into one of the so-called Jewish buildings, marked by a yellow star. She tried to flee but was captured and transported to Auschwitz from where she never emerged.'

Gladys gasped and buried her face in an embroidered handkerchief. Katalin leaned towards her and patted her hand.

'I'm so sorry. I hoped I wouldn't find her name on the lists, but it's there in black and white. The Nazis were fanatically well organised.'

'I see,' said Gladys, sitting back heavily in her chair, her face stained with tears. 'I suspected as much, but it's hard to hear. What happened to Jozsef?'

'I'm uncertain. Unfortunately, we must presume the Nazis shot him when he couldn't work any longer. They simply replaced dead workers with fresh labour.'

'My poor father. They were such beasts.'

Katalin nodded and waited until Gladys calmed herself a little. She stood up and walked over to the counter.

'I am truly sorry I haven't got better news for you. There's something else I need to tell you. The records showed we held a box of items that survived your mother's death. The same cousin who told Erzsébet about the Cooks survived the war and handed in this box of belongings in case anyone ever came to claim it. When I tried to collect it for you, I found that someone had already claimed it.'

'Who?' whispered Gladys.

'It says here the box was claimed by Joy Wells, the granddaughter of Erzsébet Steinberg and daughter of Miriam.'

'Joy visited the archive?' Gladys searched for my hand and hung on like a drowning woman. 'When did she take the box?'

Katalin checked her iPad again.

'Last week,' she said. 'She spoke to my colleague, and he gave her the items. I'm really sorry. But can't you ask your daughter to show you the belongings?'

Gladys gulped and bit her lip.

'I gave her away at birth and I only found her last month. I didn't tell her who I was and now she's missing. I've lost everyone in my whole family. Past and present.'

'But she was looking for you. That's why she came here. She said she had discovered her parents were Hungarian Jews.'

'Really? How extraordinary.'

'Be patient. She'll turn up. I'm just happy to get your stolen past back for you. Sometimes there is nothing left except the name on a Nazi list for Auschwitz. You are lucky, even if it doesn't seem like it right now.'

'You do amazing work,' I said. 'But it must take its toll.'

She sighed.

'We lost two entire generations of our family to the Nazis, and I have no photographs of anyone. That's why I do this job. I love to reunite people who are lost.'

She hesitated, and I thought she might say something else, but she shook her head at some memory and stayed silent.

We filed out of the museum into a sharp rain shower, which drenched us in no time. Gladys did not speak, even to remark upon the weather, which spoke volumes about the trauma she was processing. An enticing smell of coffee and pastries lured us into a café, and Harry made Gladys drink sweet tea and eat custard tarts for her shock. Slowly, she re-inflated and even complained about the rain. I nuzzled his damp neck and thanked my lucky stars for his big heart. Sometimes kindness is a superpower.

'Chin up, Gladys old girl. You are both looking for each other. You are bound to meet up eventually.'

'But why was Sophia murdered? You're forgetting that Joy may be in danger. We have to find her soon.'

Gladys did not reappear that evening for supper, so Harry and I tried out Felix by the riverbank. The food was delicious, but I could hardly swallow it. Harry seemed sunk into a deep depression after our visit to the museum.

'Evil didn't die with the Nazis,' he said. 'There's something odd going on. Where can Joy have disappeared to?'

'I'm stumped. I assumed we'd have leads by now. What was in the box? Did it have anything to do with Joy's disappearance or is it just a red herring?'

'The two things may be unrelated. Ryan said she came here to research her family. She only disappeared when Ryan warned her about Sophia's death.'

'Should we return to the bookshop and talk to the owner with Gladys? What if he kept secrets from us because he was protecting Joy?'

'Now that's a good call. We should go tomorrow, if she's feeling up to it.'

Our waitress came over to see if we wanted anything else to eat and the light behind her showed up the prominent round bump under her loose shirt.

'You're pregnant?' I said. 'Standing all day must be tiring.'

She smiled and patted her tummy.

'Oh, it's not so bad. I didn't even get morning sickness.'

When she had gone to get the bill, Harry turned to me.

'I didn't even notice. You have eagle eyes.'

'I'm an amateur detective. I pick up on things like that.'

When we got back to our hotel room, I slumped in a chair and scrolled through my messages. Mouse had sent one asking me to call him. I checked my watch and then remembered England would be an hour behind Budapest. Not too late to call then.

'Hi darling. I got your message. What's up?'

'I found Sandor.'

I sat bolt upright.

'Are you serious?'

'Yes. He's in a nursing home in Eastbourne. He changed his name to Sandy Forrest.'

'No wonder George couldn't trace him. Have you told your father yet?'

'Yes, I called him earlier. He's going to send Joe Brennan to the home and tell him about Sophia.'

'Poor Sandor. But he may know why Sophia, or Joy, were targeted.'

'Do you still think it's related to the Cold War?'

'I'm not sure. We've been off on a tangent since Gladys arrived. Your research proved vital for discovering what happened to her birth parents.'

I told him about Jozsef and Erzsébet and their contact with the Cooks through Erzsébet's cousin. I could almost hear him digesting the news.

'The archivist told us Joy had visited before us and took away a box containing their belongings. Gladys is frantic about it.'

'But that means Joy is still alive. She should be happy.'

'It's means she was alive last week, but unfortunately, we don't yet have a single clue leading to Joy's whereabouts. I'm not sure how much longer we'll be here if we don't dig one up.'

'I'm sure you'll find something soon. You'll probably bump into her in the street.'

'Well done on finding Sandor. At least one of us has had success.'

'Thanks Mum. I'm definitely coming home for half term, so I'll see you then.'

Afterwards, I got into bed and held Harry close. I absorbed the heat from his warm body and matched my breathing with his. Soon, we were both asleep.

Chapter 16

The next morning, my mobile phone vibrated before I had woken, and I grabbed it to stop the noise. It took me a moment to realise George was speaking to me.

'Tan, are you listening?'

'George, Isn't it rather early over there? What's up?'

'I couldn't sleep. I have news about the robbery at your shop.'

'Really. That's great news.'

'We checked the CCTV from the Surfusion camera, and we caught someone red-handed jimmying the door. He wore a hoody, but he didn't spot the camera across the road, and we got a good look at his face.'

'That's fantastic.'

'He's a known felon. He steals for hire, normally from art galleries and stately homes. Joe Brennan has taken a squad car to pick him up at his flat. He works at night, so he's not an early riser. We're sure to catch him in bed. We'll put him in a cell for a few hours to soften him up.'

'Like me. Will you question him today?'

'If we catch him. Is there anything particular you want to ask him?'

'No. The person who hired him is the one I want to question. Can you find out if he wanted anything specific from my shop? I have my suspicions.'

'Will do. Joe is going to Eastbourne this afternoon to interview Sandor. I'll let you know how it goes. Any news about Joy yet?'

'She's here somewhere. She visited the Holocaust archives last week and removed a box of items belonging to Gladys's parents. I don't think it has anything to do with Sophia's death, but there might be a connection, so we're going to follow it up.'

'Is the box connected with Sophia?'

'I don't think so. I'm working on the hypothesis someone killed her by mistake, instead of Joy.'

'Well, we're still working on the domestic violence angle here. I should have the phone data from Sophia's mobile soon. That may tell us if she was in contact with Joy. Let's stay in touch. I'll update you on Joe's visit tomorrow.'

Harry didn't mind being woken early. He never refused a meal and the breakfasts at the café were magnificent. I put my hair in a bun and took a quick shower before throwing on some clothes. Harry laughed at my speed.

'Someone's hungry,' he said.

'Hungry for information. I think we're about to have a breakthrough in our search for Joy.'

'That would be fantastic. I definitely think the bookseller could know more than he lets on.'

'We'll go to see him after breakfast.'

'I'll wake Gladys while you shower.'

After a quick breakfast, we set out for Imre's bookshop. Gladys rushed ahead of us like a clockwork mouse in her eagerness to get there. Imre Szabo arrived at his shop about five minutes after we did. He frowned when he recognised us, but his expression changed when he noticed Gladys. She had planned an entire speech to make him trust us and spill the beans about Joy. But she didn't need to ask Imre for help. Astonishment registered on his face when she walked into his shop. He rushed up and took her face in his hands, gazing at her until Gladys stepped away embarrassed by his closeness. He threw his hands in the air with excitement.

'You are Joy's mother, is it not so? I can't believe it. She will be so happy. She has searched for years.'

He kissed me and shook Harry's hand. 'This is amazing. Where did you find her?'

Gladys stared at him as if he had gone mad.

'I wasn't lost,' she said. 'I was adopted from Budapest by an English couple and brought up there. Joy and I live in the same town as Tanya and Harry in England.'

Imre looked thunderstruck.

'But she thinks she will find you in Hungary.'

'Well, I'm here now. Have you heard from her?'

'I haven't, but I think she left town to search for someone on an old collective farm near Budapest.'

'What's that?' said Harry.

'The communists who took over after the Nazis made all the farmers give up their land and work together to produce food. It was a disaster. Many people starved.'

'Which village did she go to?' I said.

'I'm sorry. I have no idea. But she left a box with me for safekeeping. It may contain clues to her whereabouts.'

'Is that the box she received from the Holocaust museum?' I asked.

'Perhaps. I never asked her for explanations. She didn't offer them either.'

'Did she mention being followed?'

'Nobody could follow Joy. Her nickname was the shadow. She never worried about that. Wait here and I'll get the box for you.'

Imre disappeared upstairs, where he could be heard shuffling across the floor above our heads. A large thud was followed by the sound of swearing and eventually he materialised holding an old shoebox.

'This is it. I expect it will be an emotional experience for you,' he said, handing it to Gladys.

'Have you seen the contents?' she asked.

'Joy told me it contains photographs of her grandparents, as well as other items.'

'My parents?' Gladys grabbed the box and held it close against her chest. 'I can't believe it. Are you sure?'

'I can open it now if you like.'

'No, don't do that. I want to open this box alone if that's alright. I must return to the hotel.'

'Of course. It's your box. You can do whatever you like.'

Tears ran down Gladys's cheeks, but her eyes were shining.

'It's a miracle. I've never seen a photograph of them. I had resigned myself to never knowing what they looked like.'

'I'm happy for you,' said Imre. 'History will speak to you from this box. Let me know if you need help. I would do anything for Joy. She is a heroine. Many people owe their lives to her.'

'She's quite an enigma,' I said. 'Thank you, Mr Szabo.'

'Take my card. You can call me if you need any help. Perhaps you will want to visit the outskirts of Budapest? I own a car and would be happy to drive you.'

'That's a wonderful offer,' said Harry. 'We'll take you up on it, but may we call you if we decide to go?'

'Of course.'

Gladys made us take her directly to the hotel where she shut herself into her room. I had a feeling we wouldn't see her again that day, so I persuaded Harry to come to the Gellert Turkish Baths with me. My guidebook told me bathing in the Gellert springs was like taking a bath in an Art Nouveau cathedral. It was not an exaggeration. From its stained-glass roof to the sky-blue pillars with cherubs and the decorative fountains, the baths were quite stunning. Harry pretended to be horrified by the price, but the moment we sunk beneath the hot geothermal waters all the stress evaporated from our bodies. I almost fell asleep under the arched glass roof surrounded by the neo-classical pillars holding up the balcony overlooking the baths.

For a couple of hours, we forgot all about Joy and Gladys and the death of Sophia Forrest and behaved like a couple on a weekend break. When we finally dragged ourselves away from the baths, we had a lovely meal in the Hotel Gellert, which completely blew our budget.

'We can't charge this to Ryan,' said Harry.

'I think we can afford one nice dinner on the Vintage,' I said. 'Anyway, I've still got that icon I gave to Ryan. I bet that will pay for dinner.'

Chapter 17

The next morning, we were woken by a gentle tapping at the door of our hotel room. I opened it to find Gladys standing there with the box she received from Imre under her arm. She looked weary, but I sensed a hidden excitement which immediately infected me. Harry came out of the bathroom wrapped in a tiny towel and did a comic double-take before retreating. I think he had plans for me. Gladys giggled.

'I think I interrupted something,' she said. 'Shall I come back later?'

'Oh, I shouldn't worry. Military men are always ready for action. I've been dying to discover what the box contained since last night.'

'It's full of priceless treasures, including a picture of my parents. I've never seen them before. I'm so emotional.'

'Why don't we have breakfast in the usual place, and you can show us everything?'

'That sounds wonderful. I needed some privacy last night to get my head around my hidden past, but now I'm absolutely starving.'

'Let's meet downstairs in half an hour,' I said.

We were soon settled at the café at a corner table where we could examine the contents of the box without getting in the way or being overlooked. Harry sat with his back to the wall 'to keep an eye out' while Gladys and I sifted through the Steinbergs' belongings.

'Let's see the photographs,' I said.

She picked out a black-and-white photograph with gentle fingers and gazed at it, crooning. Her parents looked out at us, frozen in time, half-smiles failing to hide the burden they carried. Erzsébet had a thick braid of brown hair coiled on her head and she wore a work pinafore of some sort. Jozsef had his hair slicked to one side with Brylcreem or a Hungarian equivalent. His thin face and wiry body spoke of long hours fashioning beautiful furniture in his workshop. Baby Gladys peeped over the top of a crocheted blanket, her snub nose impertinent and still recognisable.

'I look like my mother,' said Gladys.

'She was beautiful,' I said, feeling tearful.

I looked at the photograph again. Something bothered me about it, but I couldn't put my finger on it. Gladys took it back and held it to her heart.

'I never imagined I'd find out what they looked like. It's the most amazing feeling. Of course, they wouldn't be alive anymore, even if they had escaped to England, but I finally feel as if they're real.'

'I'm so happy for you,' said Harry, his voice catching in his throat. 'Now we've got to find the next generation.'

Before it's too late lingered unsaid. Gladys put the photograph down and retrieved another from the box.

'This is the photograph Magda gave me. The one that somebody sent to Joy of a man holding two babies. I'm pretty sure that man is also my father. If you put the photographs side by side, the similarity is striking, even though one is rather blurred. Can you see what I mean?'

'You're right. It looks like him.'

'So whose babies are those?' said Harry.

I picked up the photograph of her parents and looked closely at it.

'Are there more photographs of your parents?'

'Yes, one more of my mother, but it's blurred too.'

'May I see it?'

Gladys sorted through the papers in the box and gave me the photograph. A woman stood in the half light of open curtains. She had her hand on her stomach, which bulged a little in her dress. The revelation I experienced the night before returned.

'Is it possible she's pregnant?'

'Pregnant? Oh my heavens. You might be right,' she said.

'What if your mother had another child after you were sent away?' I asked.

'Another child? You mean a brother or sister? But why didn't Katalin tell us about them?' said Harry.

I remembered Katalin's slight hesitation before we left the museum that day. Could she be hiding information from us?

'I think we should pay another visit to the archives.'

'A sibling?' said Gladys, who seemed to have entered a trance state. 'I have a sister or brother?'

'There are two babies in that photo of your father,' I said. 'You may have had twin siblings. But we don't know for sure. They might not have survived the war. Or still be alive.'

'But they'd be younger than me,' said Gladys. 'Did Katalin hid the truth from me?'

'It's possible.'

'But why would she do that?'

'She may have wanted to protect you,' said Harry, putting on his army voice. 'Finish your breakfast, Gladys. You need your strength. It may be bad news, or a false lead. Please don't get your hopes up too high.'

We sat in shellshocked silence as they brought our breakfast. Gladys kept muttering 'I can't believe it' to herself. I couldn't think of anything to comfort her. I found it almost impossible to eat much owing to the lump in my throat. Even Harry seemed to struggle. Finally, we gave up any attempt to finish our food. Harry paid for our meal and had to assure the staff that everything had been delicious when they saw the food left on our plates.

We headed for the Jewish museum once again with a renewed sense of purpose. Gladys walked beside Harry, carrying the box in a plastic bag. After a tense walk, we arrived at the archives to find Katalin speaking to another family, all of whom were weeping. Her stoic reaction to the sea of tears made me even more certain of my theory. Anyone who had to deal with tragedy every day might think it harmless to conceal secrets which would cause more upset. She had one of the saddest jobs in the world, removing the last vestiges of hope about family reunions. She glanced up at us and alarm showed on her face when she noticed our steely determination. Rumbled.

'I didn't expect to see you again,' she said, when the other family had departed. 'Did you forget something?'

'No, but you did,' said Gladys, handing her the photograph of her father holding the two babies. 'Am I wrong in thinking I had brothers?'

Katalin bit her lip and sighed.

'I wanted to spare you worse grief,' she said. 'I thought you had lost enough already. Sometimes the burden of telling people awful truths all day gets too much.'

'What happened to them?'

'Your mother hid the boys with the Schmidt family on a farm outside of Budapest after they were born. When they shipped Erzsébet to Auschwitz, the twins were left behind. One baby died of typhus soon afterwards. The other boy disappeared. It is likely he died too. The farm was taken into a collective and conditions were awful. Your mother gave a letter to the family before she was taken, with the details of the Cooks, and the list of valuables sent to England, in case she ever escaped.'

'Are the family still alive?'

'Possibly. They weren't Jewish, so if they got enough to eat, they may have survived. The older generation are gone now, but their children may be alive.'

'Can you give us the address?' I asked.

Katalin frowned.

'Yes, but I think you'll be disappointed. Most collective farms were deserted after the communist era.'

'Anything is worth a try,' said Gladys.

Katalin scribbled the address on a piece of paper and handed it over. Gladys secreted it in her handbag.

'Thank you. I don't hold it against you. I just need to know.'

'Forgive me if I made things worse instead of better.'

'You're a brave young woman. You do a horrible job with grace. I'm very grateful for the photos and the information.'

'What was the family's name?' asked Harry.
'Schmidt.'

'And the names of my brothers?' said Gladys.

'Jozsef and Janos. They were born about three months after you were sent to England. So they would have been toddlers when the Schmidts fostered them.'

'Where did they live?'

'In Solymar, northwest of Budapest. I'm sorry, but I don't have any further information about them on file.'

Gladys stood up on shaky legs.

'I know you did it with the best of intentions, so I don't hold it against you, but I don't think I can bear to spend another minute here.'

She tottered out, and I rushed after her while Harry poured oil on the troubled waters. I found Gladys leaning against a wall. Harry took her by the arm, gently hauling her to her feet.

'Let's leave this place,' he said.

Chapter 18

We emerged from the Jewish museum into the sunlight with no coherent plan. Gladys seemed shellshocked. She held onto Joy's box and could not be parted from it. I couldn't blame her after the news she had received. Harry led us to the same café we had visited on a previous visit to the archives. He ordered coffee and cake for us and made Gladys sit down in a comfortable chair. She had a strange expression on her face, stubborn and unyielding. I put three sugars in her coffee and gave it to her. She crashed it back on the saucer.

'I won't be beaten,' she said. 'My daughter's out there somewhere and I'm going to find her. Have you got Imre's card with you?'

Harry nodded and fished it out of his wallet.

'Can you ask him to drive us to Solymar? Now.'

'He might be busy,' I said. 'Perhaps—'

'He won't be too busy to rescue Joy.'

She folded her arms, looking almost comically stern. I lent Harry my mobile phone, and he dialled Imre's number.

'Hello? Imre? It's Harry Fletcher here. You offered to take us to that farm Joy mentioned? We've got the name of the town and—'

'Right away? Yes, we're in the café having coffee. Can we get one for you? Okay. See you shortly.'

'What did he say?' asked Gladys.

'He's coming here immediately.'

'Didn't I tell you?' she said with a smug smile. 'He'd do anything for my girl.'

Imre turned up ten minutes later with a bag full of pastries and a flask he filled with tea at the counter. I gave him one of my tea bags, as I knew Joy would be desperate for a cuppa. I didn't allow myself to wonder if we would find her, or if she would be alive.

We piled into Imre's car. Harry up front with Imre, and Gladys and me in the backseat.

'Where are we going?' said Imre.

'Solymar,' said Gladys.

'I've been there often,' said Imre. 'The Commonwealth War Cemetery is in that village. It contains the graves of airmen who died in Hungary during the second world war.'

'What nationality are they?' asked Harry.

'Mostly British, and some Canadians, Australians, South Africans and Polish, all members of the RAF. It's a wonderful tribute to their sacrifice.'

Harry didn't speak again during our brief journey through the north-eastern outskirts of Budapest. I could sense him brooding. He always took the death of any service personnel to heart, even those in the distant past.

Soon we were driving through the countryside into the village of Solymar. The roads were lined with beautiful mature sycamore and ash trees, their panoply of green leaves bright in the sunlight.

'There are some beautiful waterfalls in the Solymar area,' said Imre. 'Many prosperous people moved out of Budapest to live here in the nineteen-nineties. They occupied the empty homes left by the Germans who were deported.'

'Germans?' said Gladys. 'You mean Nazis?'

'No, the people deported were descendants of settlers from Bavaria who came to restore the farmlands along the Danube. About half the population of Solymar returned to Germany in nineteen-forty-six as part of the scheme to deport ethnic Germans from eastern European countries.'

'Wow, that seems a little harsh,' I said.

'What about their treatment of the Jews?' said Gladys. 'I'd like to go to the cemetery first, Imre. We may find my brothers there.'

She folded her arms again. I didn't argue. There seemed little point with her mood. Imre pulled up beside the graveyard and we all got out.

'We can review a row of graves each until we find the Schmidts,' said Harry.

'That sounds good,' I said.

It didn't take long before Imre shouted at us to join him in front of a gravestone with several names inscribed onto it.

'From the dates, I'd say these are the Schmidt grandparents of that era, but here below is the name of your brother, Jozsef.'

Gladys knelt on the ground with difficulty and pulled out some weeds, which had covered the lettering. Gently, she touched the inscription with her hand. A tear ran down her cheek and hung on her chin like an opaque crystal.

'He was only four years old. What does the inscription say?' I asked.

'It says sleeps with the angels,' said Imre.

'But where's Janos?' I said. 'Shouldn't he be here if he died? And the Schmidt parents are missing too.'

'Perhaps no one remained to make the inscriptions,' said Harry.

A cough behind us made us jump. An ancient priest stood on the path supported by a Zimmer frame. He spoke to Imre in Hungarian first, but then he addressed Gladys in halting English.

'You are the sister of Jozsef and Janos? What a coincidence. I knew the Schmidt family when I was a small boy. I used to go to their farm to buy milk.' He gazed into the past and he sighed. We waited for him to speak again.

'You've found Jozsef, I see. Those poor little boys. Despite their age, Franz Schmidt had them outside weeding in all weathers from morning to night. They were so skinny; a wind could have knocked them over. My mother used to give me bread rolls for them, but Mr Schmidt caught me feeding the boys one day and he walloped me and them.'

'How did Jozsef die?' I asked.

The priest frowned and his hands tightened on his Zimmer frame.

'The Schmidts blamed typhus, but my mother told me he died of starvation. He was the eldest, you see. He used to give his food to Janos. I think it killed him.'

Gladys sobbed into her handkerchief and the priest patted her on the shoulder, his face contorted with remorse.

'I'm sorry,' he said. 'I couldn't save him.'

'But you were only a little boy. What could you have done?' said Harry. 'What happened after Jozsef died?'

'Oh, the family being ethnic Germans, they were forced out during the deportations.'

Gladys visibly deflated. 'You don't know what happened to them?'

'I didn't. But there's a Jonas Kovacs who moved to town last year. He might know. He owns the old Schmidt Farmhouse. It's deserted now of course.'

'Can you give us directions?'

It turned out the farmhouse was about two kilometres away, so we used Imre's car. Mr Kovacs's house sat about three hundred yards from the old farm building. A smart modern house of a decent size with regimented floral borders and pristine paving stones, which lead to a newly painted black front door. I noticed the complete lack of weeds and had a horrible feeling of déjà vu. Imre knocked on the door and we waited on tenterhooks for somebody to answer. Gladys grabbed my hand again.

'I don't think my heart will survive the stress of the last few days,' she said. 'I'm so tired and sad.'

'Hang in there. Joy needs you.'

The door opened a crack, and a thin, pale woman peeped out. She looked frightened. Imre spoke to her in a quiet voice but only managed a few questions before she shut the door again, shaking her head.

'What did she say?' I asked.

'Her husband left for work a few days ago and she's not sure when he's coming back. He's been travelling a lot recently.'

'Could she tell you anything about the Schmidt family farm?'

'I got the impression she's petrified of her husband. She told me she knew nothing about this place,' said Imre.

'There may be someone else in town who can give us information.'

'Possibly,' said Harry. 'Why don't we search around the old farmhouse? You never know what we might find. People probably left on foot when they were rounded up and forced to leave. They may have had to abandon papers and photographs.'

We walked down the hill to the farm and entered the cobbled yard. Despite the dilapidated state of the buildings, I could spot traces of recent activity especially near the house. Someone had barricaded the door with a newly cut piece of wood stuck in two metal brackets. I screwed up my eyes and tried to see through the mud and cobwebs into the cottage's gloomy interior. To my astonishment, I saw a modern plastic bottle on the kitchen table.

'We have to enter,' I said to Harry. 'I think somebody may be inside.'

Harry and Imre used rocks to shift the log jamming the door closed, and Gladys ran inside calling for Joy. No one answered.

'Spread out and check the other rooms,' said Harry. 'I'll go with Gladys.'

Imre and I climbed up the creaky staircase into the eaves and investigated the tight space under the roof. Some cardboard boxes whose contents had spilled out sat on the floor. They appeared to be charts recording milk production, but they had two columns where each daily result was reduced between the first and the second. I showed them to Imre. He grinned.

'It looks as if the farmers were cooking the books,' he said. 'When the communists took over in Hungary, they forced farmers to join collectives by consolidating individual farms. This process was met with resistance, mostly passive, like lying about the real production statistics of the cooperative. This provided people more to eat and even extra to sell outside the system. They were hard times. People were always hungry.'

'Who made these charts?' I asked.

'Not Mr Schmidt. His name doesn't appear anywhere. I guess the priest had it right. He got deported with the other ethnic Germans.'

We descended again and found Harry rolling his eyes at Gladys who crawled under the table. She emerged with a scrap of paper, waving it in triumph.

'Joy was here. This is a receipt from the Shanty. I recognise the logo.'

'What does it say?' said Imre.

'It's torn off, but it says, "Germany? I need to tell…" That's all.'

'It doesn't help much,' said Harry.

'We know she was here. She must be following the same line of thinking as you. But where is she now?' said Imre.

'I'd like to bet Kovacs had something to do with her disappearance,' I said.

'Ah, but did he kidnap her, or help her? We can't tell yet,' said Harry.

'We must be close. I found some bread on the counter and mould hadn't grown on it yet.'

'What do we do next?' said Imre.

'I can't speak for you lot, but I'm going to the War Cemetery to catch up with the RAF lads,' said Harry. 'You don't have to come too. I won't be long.'

'I'd like to go,' I said.

'Me too,' said Gladys

'I've been there often,' said Imre. 'But I'd like to go again. I'll collect the car and park outside.'

He headed off up the road while we did the short walk to the entrance. A small metal gateway led inside the graveyard, which was surrounded by a low stone wall and massive chestnut trees in bloom. Four sections around a central monument had been set out in rows. Most of the gravestones were made from similar white marble with rounded tops. We stopped just inside the gate to read a register of the graves which had been inscribed with the name, rank and family details of the fallen heroes. Then we wandered down the rows of the dead, reading the heartbreaking dedications to each pilot. Crew members from the same flight were buried side by side, making it still more poignant. Friends and crew mates in life were neighbours in death. Some inscriptions made me quite tearful. Their sacrifice, so final and so brave, made me wonder if we could find the courage to stand up too, even in this different age.

'They gave their tomorrow that we might have our today,' said Harry, his voice rough with emotion.

'The oldest man here is thirty-six,' said Gladys. 'They were babies.'

We stood silently together, gazing at the rows of white marble tombstones. Only when Imre arrived at our side did we move again.

'Brave men,' he said. 'Let's find our brave woman.'

Chapter 19

We returned to Budapest where Imre invited us into his shop to discuss our findings. Gladys sank into an armchair and fell asleep almost immediately. Harry covered her with his jacket. She looked younger and defenceless curled up in the chair. Imre smiled at the sight.

'She's amazing isn't she? How old is she? '

'We haven't asked, but she came to England as a baby in nineteen thirty-nine, so it's easy to work out,' I said.

'What did we discover today?' said Harry.

'Janos Steinberg probably survived the war and got taken to Germany,' I said. 'And a man called Jonas Kovacs has bought the Schmidt's farm at Solymar and may have met Joy,' said Imre.

'Could they be the same person?' I said. 'Although why would Janos return to a place that he hated? I must ask Mouse to research the history of the Schmidts of Solymar.'

'That piece of paper in the cottage is certainly intriguing. Kovacs may have caught her nosing around and thrown her out,' said Imre.

'It would explain the barricaded door,' said Harry.

'I keep coming back to the Steinberg's box of belongings,' I said. 'Katalin told us the other archivist had given it to Joy. What if they also had a visit from Kovacs? What if he was searching for Gladys?'

'I could find out the second archivist's name,' said Imre. 'We could return to the Archive when he or she is on duty. It's possible Joy told them what she planned to do next.'

'I should call Joy's husband Ryan and update him on our progress, or lack of it. At least we found evidence of Joy being alive. That's a positive development.'

'It was a scrap of paper. It proves nothing. We don't know how long it lay there,' said Harry.

'It can't have lain there long. Joy only came to Hungary recently.'

'I know Joy kept photographs in the box. Did she leave anything else that might have relevance?' said Imre.

'I didn't have time to review the whole box. We were so shocked with the revelation about the twins, we set out immediately for the archives to question Katalin.'

'Where is it now?'

'Gladys had it.'

'It's not here now. She could have left it in your car,' I said.

Imre stood up and headed for his vehicle. He didn't run, but he looked as if he wanted to. He opened the car's back door and peered in. Then he searched the whole car with increasing urgency. He came back inside, panting with exertion.

'It's not there,' he said. 'Someone must have removed it.'

'But when? We'd have seen anyone who opened the door while we were sitting here.'

'When we searched the farmhouse, we left the car beside the Kovacs' house,' I said. 'What if Mrs Kovacs searched the car while we searched the farm?'

'We've got to return to Solymar,' said Harry. 'Right now.'

'What about Gladys?'

'Can you stay and guard her? Imre and I can deal with Mrs Kovacs.'

'But can you force her to confess?'

'I work for MI6, remember?'

Harry snorted into his hand, trying not to wake Gladys who merely whimpered and continued sleeping.

'Hurry back,' he said. 'Don't take any risks.'

We set out again on the short drive. Imre's hands were tight on the steering wheel. I wondered if he had a crush on Joy. He seemed too invested in her safety as a neutral colleague. It took half an hour to return to the Kovacs' house. The curtains were pulled shut as we got out.

'How do we play this?' said Imre. 'It's not as if we have any authority here.'

I smirked at him and reached into my handbag to take out my fake MI6 pass. His eyes were like saucers when I opened it for him to see.

'Wow! I didn't realise you were a spook too. How come Joy never showed me hers?'

'I'll tell you later. Let's give Mrs Kovacs a fright. Tell her I'm from the British secret service and the documents she stole are top secret. Pretend if she doesn't give them back, we will take her into custody and deport her to the UK for trial. I'll hold up the card behind you and look stern.'

It worked like clockwork. Mrs Kovacs almost fainted when I flashed my MI6 pass. Imre translated their conversation, and I kept a straight face through most of it. She told him her husband had ordered her to search any suspicious car in case we were thieves intending to steal from the farm. He had asked her to take any papers she found and keep it for his return, and she had already texted him to say she had the box. She begged Imre to let her keep it or her husband might kill her in a rage.

'Did she inform him of the contents?'

'Not yet.'

'We can take out the photographs and keepsakes and leave the administrative stuff. Does she have a photocopier?' I asked.

She nodded.

'Tell her she can keep the originals until her husband sees them, but she must make us copies of anything we want now.'

She pulled us indoors and led us to what seemed to be Kovacs's study. She would not enter, but stood at the door, exhorting Imre to be careful and not touch anything except the copier. A large oak desk took up most of the room, with a dust free space where a laptop had recently been removed. A flat cap hung on a hook, but no other personal items humanised the room. I removed the photographs and a few trinkets from the box, but the contents were mostly documents and theatre tickets and things of no value. Then I saw a few yellowing pieces of papers held together with a rusty staple. A list of items written with a fountain pen in a neat hand covered one sheet and the other had details of Gladys's age, date and place of birth and her physical characteristics including a small birthmark on her right shoulder.

'Look at this. I think it's the list of the treasures given to the Cook sisters to back up Gladys's visa.'

'Read it,' said Imre.

I held the fragile paper with care as I reviewed the list. The items included gold jewellery, silver hair clips, three rough diamonds of moderate size, two hundred pounds sterling, which must have been obtained on the black market, a small painting and some clip earrings. Gladys's family legacy may have been dispersed years ago. Had Mabel Fitch sold everything when she realised the Steinbergs were never coming to collect their daughter?

'I wonder if Gladys is the key to this mystery?' I said.

'I don't see how. Unless she also worked as an agent during the Cold War,' said Imre. 'I've finished copying everything. Shall we get on the road again?'

I noticed Mrs Kovacs's expression. Fear leaked out of every pore on her face.

'Ask her what's wrong,' I said.

Imre spoke to her, and she pointed at the pile of paper and tears fell on her blouse. He reached into his pocket and took some bills out of his wallet. She looked pathetically grateful.

As we left the house, I asked him about the money.

'Oh, she said her husband would notice if the paper was missing and he counts every penny she spends. She wanted cash to replace the paper, so he didn't notice it's missing.'

'What about the number of copies?'

'I told her to switch off the copier and reset it. She can pretend there was a power cut.'

I looked back at the house and its twitching curtains. Mr Kovacs had a coercive relationship with his wife, but we couldn't help her. I felt wretched, but

Imre didn't look back. He handed me the pile of papers and got back into his car.

'What do we tell Gladys?'

'I think she'd swap pieces of paper to see her daughter again,' he said. 'Joy is in danger. We've got to figure out the mystery before something bad happens to her.'

When we got back to the shop, Harry and Gladys had disappeared. I checked my mobile phone and found Harry had sent me a message telling me they had gone back to the hotel to rest. Imre offered to drive me to the hotel, but I wanted some time to myself to consider the day's developments. I hadn't expected to find the list of items taken to England by the Cooks. I wondered if Gladys still had any of them in her possession. She had never talked about her past until Joy had disappeared. Maybe she held the key to the mystery.

Harry opened the door of our room and enveloped me in his muscly arms. His smell of soap and toast made me want to bottle it for sale. I snuggled into his chest and sighed with contentment.

'Don't get too comfortable,' he said. 'We need to do a debrief.'

'Okay,' I said, dropping my coat on the floor and slipping my shirt over my head.

'Not that sort of debrief,' he said, but I ignored him. Sometimes you need a break from MI6.

Chapter 20

Gladys knocked on our door a couple of hours later, waking us from our nap. I yawned widely and stared at her through bleary eyes.

'Hi there. How are you holding up?'

She took in my dishevelled state and put her hands on her hips.

'As well as expected. Did you get my box back?'

'Sort of. Some of the most precious things like photographs, but some we photocopied to stop Schmidt assaulting his wife.'

'Have you got them here?'

'The photographs and the Cooks' list are in my handbag, but the rest of the box is back in Imre's attic. I need to talk to you about the list.'

'I'm starving. Why don't we eat dinner and we can try to make sense of what we saw today?'

'Should we invite Imre?' said Harry.

'He told me he had to sort out a large delivery of books tonight. We should see him tomorrow?'

'I'll see you both in the lobby in fifteen minutes,' said Gladys.

'Make it twenty,' I said.

Twenty-two minutes later, we discovered Gladys pacing the lobby like an expectant father. I couldn't help guffawing at her hangry face. Harry slipped his arm through hers and swanned out to the street.

'Where are we going?' said Gladys.

'0,75 Bar and Bistro,' said Harry.

'Only three-quarters of a restaurant?' said Gladys. 'I'm really quite hungry you know.'

It didn't take us long to walk back to St Stephen's Square. We got a table straight away and ordered a bottle of wine.

'The smell of the food is making me crazy,' said Gladys. 'Tell them to bring the breadbasket right away.'

I was surprised how chipper she was, despite the sobering news about the twins. I guessed she had cried herself dry before coming out to dinner. Gladys was made of stern stuff. Her generation didn't believe in outward displays of emotion. We ordered our food and asked the waiter to bring it as soon as possible, before Gladys started biting the other clients. The waiter laughed, but I wasn't trying to be funny. I felt the buzz of my mobile phone in my handbag and took it out.

'You're not going to scroll during dinner, are you?' said Harry, who only used his phone for calls and texts.

'No, it's an urgent message from George. He wants me to call him right back. I'll take it outside.'

Before they could protest, I weaved my way through the tables and stood outside in the cool night air. I almost stood on an alley cat who hissed at me, making me jump, and disappeared into the shadows before I could react. My phone bounced out of my hand and landed in an artificial hedge. I dug around until I felt its smooth edges and pulled it out. I had a vision of Hades sitting in the Grotty Hovel waiting for us and felt homesick. Helen, my sister, fed him twice a day, but he wasn't grateful. I had several photographs on my WhatsApp feed of Hades sulking in the garden. I dialled George's number still feeling nostalgic.

'Where have you been?'

'We were out of town today. I—'

'Honestly, why are you gallivanting about when there's police work to be done?'

I almost reminded him he wasn't married to me anymore, and I was not, in fact, a detective, but I let that ride.

'What's so important?'

'Sandor's dead.'

'That's unfortunate, but he must have been in his eighties, right? It's not surprising.'

'He didn't die of natural causes. He's been dead for weeks. Murdered.'

'Murdered? Are you sure?'

'Is the Pope a catholic?'

'Okay. But how?'

'Tortured and suffocated. Someone crept into his room at lunchtime and killed him while everyone was eating.'

A chill ran up my spine.

'Did DI Antrim tell you this?'

'Yes, Joe spoke to him when the staff at the care home told him about the murder.'

I didn't see any point in telling him I already knew about the murder. I wondered if we had put two and two together sooner would Sophia still be alive. A dreadful thought.

'Are you still there?'

'Yes, I'm sorry. How horrible. Can we trace the murderer?'

'There may be some CCTV footage from the car park. Terry Antrim is going to chase it up for us. Have you got anywhere over there?'

'We know Joy had been looking for members of her family and she was alive, at least until recently, but we haven't caught up with her yet. Has Ryan heard from her?'

'Not that he's told us. Can you give him a ring? He'll tell you stuff he won't tell me.'

'What about Sophia's phone?'

'No luck yet. Apple phones are almost impossible to crack, and the backlog at digital forensics is as long as my arm. I've instigated a rush order though, so we should get the text messages in the next few days. When are you coming home?'

'I'm not sure. But now Sandor's been murdered, it seems like we may be looking in the wrong place. Oh…'

'Oh what?'

'I'll have to tell Gladys. She's had more than her fair share of bad news this week. I'm worried the strain of pretending she's fine will break her.'

'She's a tough old bird. You'll find a way. Come home soon. Hades misses you.'

How typical of my ex to use Hades to convey his feelings. Our relationship improved after we divorced. I even liked him again despite everything. I steeled myself to go back to our table. Sandor and Gladys had been divorced about fifty years, but she had been nostalgic about him since Sophia's murder. How would she take it?

'What happened?' said Harry, before I even sat down. 'Something bad. I can tell. Is Mouse okay?'

'Mouse is fine. It's Sandor. I'm so sorry Gladys. George says he's been murdered.'

'Murdered? But who would murder Sandor? Unless it's a jealous husband, but I doubt any of them are still living,' said Gladys. 'I'd have murdered him myself if I'd got the chance.'

'It can't be a coincidence,' I said. 'You need to take this seriously.'

'I'm sorry. Poor old Sandor. I'm not exactly sad he's gone, but you're right. The murder must be linked to Sophia and Joy.'

'Probably, although it happened weeks ago.'

'Weeks ago? Why didn't we hear about it earlier?'

'Sandor was using the surname Forrest, and the police didn't realise who he was at first.'

'Forrest? Oh, the surname of his second wife. How odd.'

'This whole thing feels like a personal vendetta more than some vague connection with the Cold War,' I said. 'But what? And why did Joy stay in Budapest? It seems odd with the murders being in England.'

'Maybe it seemed safer than going home,' said Harry. 'While she figured out what the motive was.'

'But she must be aware we're in Budapest by now. Why hasn't she visited us at the hotel?' said Gladys.

'That's a brilliant point,' I said. 'Perhaps it's being watched.'

'Could it be Kovacs?' said Harry.

'I doubt it. He only left home a few days ago,' I said. 'Wait a minute. Someone followed us on our first night in Budapest.'

'That was Gladys,' said Harry.

'I hadn't arrived yet,' said Gladys. 'I flew in the day after you two.'

'What if there is someone from Joy's past who is stalking her? It doesn't have to be related to her search for family. It may not be related to the murders in England.'

'Now that's plausible,' said Harry. 'Ryan said Joy had plenty of enemies, but he claimed most of them were dead. What if someone is looking for revenge?'

'That could explain why she is in hiding,' said Gladys. 'She must have a safe house, though. Perhaps it blocks signals in or out for security? Someone must know where it is.'

'Surely Ryan could ask the head office? They've got to trust him,' said Harry.

'I'll call him now,' I said. 'If he hasn't heard from her, he'll really be getting worried.'

Ryan picked up the call on the first ring. His voice betrayed his relief when he heard me speak.

'Tanya, how nice to hear from you. Have you got any news?'

'We think Joy has recently been in a village called Solymar where her uncles were left with a family after her grandmother got sent to Auschwitz.'

'Uncles? Gladys had brothers? I thought she was an only child?'

'So did she until we found a photograph of them as babies. Anyway, it seems we are always one step behind her.'

'Knowing Joy, she must be aware you are in Budapest by now. I wonder why she hasn't contacted you?'

'That's exactly what we thought. But there may be someone watching us. Does Joy have somewhere else she can go to if she suspects she's being tracked?'

'Ah, that would explain the radio silence. I believe she does, but I'm not privy to its location. We always had separate bolt holes in case one of us got captured.

That way, foreign agents couldn't force us to tell them where the other was hiding.'

'Can you remember anything which might narrow it down?'

'I think she had a bolthole underground.'

'Can you find out from head office?'

'I'll get on to it immediately.'

Chapter 21

The next morning, Magda from reception called me over as we were waiting for Gladys to come down for breakfast. She glanced from side to side and wrung her hands together. Her knuckles were white through her skin. I pretended not to notice her agitation, greeting her as usual.

'Good morning Magda. How are you today?'

'Not good. I think I saw Miss Joy this morning outside the hotel, but something scared her, and she disappeared again before I could talk to her. It's not like her to be frightened.'

'Joy was here? Are you sure?'

'Absolutely.'

Harry who had been listening, strode over to the entrance and scanned the street for danger while putting his hand out as if he was checking for rain. He soon came back inside and nodded.

'A large man wearing a flat cap is loitering behind that Doric pillar. He may be having a smoke, but there's something about him I don't like.'

'Might he be watching the hotel?' I said.

'It's easy to check, but I need bait. Are you up for it?'

I gulped.

'What do you want me to do?'

'Take Gladys along for breakfast and sit in full view of the street. I'll wait here for a few minutes and see if the chap follows you. You won't be in any danger. I'll be right behind him.'

'But what will Gladys say?'

'Tell her I'm going to be five minutes late. Don't mention the man outside and whatever you do, don't glance over at him.'

'Okay, but be careful.'

'He's not in the first flush of youth. I'll be fine. Magda, can I hide in your office for a moment?'

Magda nodded. Her face had recovered some colour from her excitement at our plan.

'Get him, Mr Fletcher. He's the one, I'm sure of it.'

Harry disappeared behind the counter and hid in Magda's office. About two minutes later, Gladys came down the stairs.

'No Harry yet?' she said, looking around.

'He'll follow us. He needed to make some calls this morning.'

'Are you sure we shouldn't wait?'

'Quite sure. Let's go.'

Gladys slipped her arm through mine.

'Girls' breakfast? Sounds good to me. We can discuss our next move. I'm getting the hang of this detective lark.'

I stifled a laugh and led her outside to the street. All my will power was required to stop me spying on the man behind the pillar. I could almost feel him watch us and then amble after us as if he was off to get a pint of milk from the local shop. Gladys squeezed my arm.

'Are you okay, dear? You feel very tense. Did you and Harry have a row?'

'Oh, no. We never fight. Well, almost never. He'll be with us shortly.'

I attempted to release the tension from my arm and swept Gladys along to the café. I asked for a table outside, but Gladys shook her head.

'Do we have to? It's parky out this morning. Let's sit inside.'

'Okay, but let's sit by the window so I can watch the birds.'

She humoured me, though there wasn't a tree in sight and the chickens in the supermarket on the corner were the only birds nearby. We ordered breakfast, and I plopped two tea bags into the jug of hot water they brought to the table. I ordered fried eggs with Hungarian sausage, and a cheese omelette with fried onions for Harry. Gladys had a chocolate swirl to satisfy her sweet tooth. The hum of conversation and the clatter of cutlery on plates filled the café. Most people drank coffee and ate cottage cheese pastries. The odour of fresh coffee filled my nostrils and tempted me, but my stomach didn't like coffee until after midmorning. I still didn't dare to turn around in case the man noticed me checking. I could only imagine Harry's face if I alerted the man that he had been rumbled.

Gladys went on about how handsome Sandor had been in his youth, and I struggled to concentrate on what she was saying. Suddenly, there was a shout, and a thud followed by a groan. After a brief scuffle, Harry appeared with a scruffy-looking man under his power. He appeared to be holding the man's arm twisted behind him. I had a feeling of déjà vu.

I jumped up, leaving Gladys mid-sentence and dashed outside.

'Do you speak English?' Harry asked him.

'A little.'

'What if I offered you the chance to explain why you are following us? I'll even buy you breakfast if you promise not to run.'

The man wriggled ineffectually and then shrugged.

'Okay.'

Harry maintained a tight grip on him until he was sitting at our table. The waitress gave him a long stare before taking his order.

'What's your name?' I asked.

'Boris Peskov.'

Harry rolled his eyes.

'Isn't that the equivalent of Peter Brown in England?'

'It's my name.'

'Why were you following us?'

'I wasn't following you. I was waiting for someone.'

'Joy Wells?' asked Gladys, narrowing her eyes.

'So?' said the man. 'It's not against the law.'

'I'm pretty sure it's illegal to stalk someone, but perhaps only in England,' I said. 'Because you must have threatened her, or Joy wouldn't have disappeared.'

'Have you hurt her?' said Harry.

'Not yet,' he said, sneering. 'But I'd like to.'

'What's she done to you?' said Gladys.

'She made a fool of me and got me fired from the service. It's payback time. She's so scared, she doesn't know what's going on. She thought her war was over, but mine isn't. This is my revenge and I'm enjoying it more than I can say.'

'Seriously? Isn't the Cold War finished?' said Harry.

The man smirked.

'Not for me.'

Harry gripped the man by the throat before he could move away. The man's eyes bulged in fright and Harry smiled like a tiger with its prey.

'It is now. I'm special forces and I have certain talents you might know about. If you come anywhere near Joy Wells again, I'd be delighted to practise the full range of them on your body. You'll disappear for good afterwards. Is stalking Joy Wells worth a horrible death?'

Boris's eyes came out on stalks. He shook himself free.

'You don't have to treat me like that. I'm a reasonable man. I have needs.'

He rubbed his thumb and index finger together.

'You want us to pay you to back off?' I said.

'Times are hard.'

'They'll be even tougher if you don't forget about your vendetta,' said Harry. 'Eat your breakfast and think yourself lucky I don't break your fingers one by one just for fun.'

The way he said it made the hairs on my arms stand on end. Sometimes I wondered exactly what Harry had done in the SAS before he retired. He had told me about his tours in Afghanistan, but I suspected the details of some of his short missions would stay secret. It certainly made Boris shut up. He said nothing else while he ate his enormous breakfast. I felt sorry for him when I saw his skinny arms and realised he hadn't lied about hard times. When he left, wrapping his coat tight around his wiry frame, I pressed the equivalent of fifty pounds into his hand. He didn't thank me but shuffled down the street, smoking the dog end of a cigarette he had been storing behind his ear.

'Will Joy know it's safe to come out of hiding?' said Gladys.

'I'm not sure it is. Just because Peskov says he'll back off doesn't mean he's telling the truth,' said Harry.

'We must keep looking for her. Sandor's death has convinced me the murderer wanted to kill Joy, not Sophia. We have no idea why,' I said.

'So, we're back at square one?' said Harry.

'It certainly feels that way.'

Chapter 22

After Boris slunk off into the sunny morning, an air of depression settled over us. We ate in silence, bar the occasional sigh from Gladys who had abandoned half of her chocolate swirl. Harry ate his omelette with the ferocity of someone who had had a massive dose of adrenaline flooding through his body a few minutes previously. I forced myself to finish my eggs, normally my favourite meal of the day, and then turned to my mobile phone for comfort. Mouse had a lot to answer for. I had never used a smart phone before he broke into the Grotty Hovel one night. He had dragged me kicking and screaming into the twenty-first century after my bout of depression had cut me off from the world for too long.

The phone rang in my hand, and I almost dropped it into my tea. George. Did he finally have a breakthrough for me?

'Tan, it's me.'

'I know. I can see your name on my screen.'

'There's no need to be catty. I've got good news.'

'Excellent. We're just finishing breakfast. Can I call you back in fifteen minutes so we can have privacy? That way I can put you on speaker phone.'

'Okay, but hurry. I have to chase up a shoplifting case. The cheeky bugger sauntered into the Co-op, loaded up his rucksack with batteries and razors from the shelves and left without paying. It's an epidemic. I think it's the same guy that beat one of the shop assistants up last week. We've got him on CCTV from that time. His hoody slipped off when they tried to stop him leaving.'

'That reminds me. Do you have any news on the break in at Second Home?'

'As a matter of fact, I do. Gather up the troops and give me a ring shortly.'

I hung up and noticed both Gladys and Harry had lifted their heads again, faces animated with excitement.

'George has news. Let's return to our room where we can listen in private.'

'Are you sure it's private?' said Harry. 'Soviet spies used to be fantastic at bugging rooms.'

Gladys rubbed her hands together with glee.

'Ooh. I feel like I'm starring in one of those black and white spy films like the Twenty-Nine Steps.'

'This resembles a book from the Smiley series,' said Harry. 'I wonder who Karla is?'

'Never mind Karla. You've got a point about the bugging. Maybe Magda can lend us a different room in the hotel?'

Magda couldn't wait to find us an empty room for the call. I considered asking her to stay, but I didn't want to put her in danger. I was thinking like Joy. Spying was addictive.

After she left, I dialled George and propped the telephone up against a lamp with the speaker at full volume. Gladys and I sat on the edge of the bed and Harry pulled up a chair. George answered.

'All present and correct?' he asked. 'Are you sitting comfortably? Then I'll begin.'

Harry guffawed.

'Listen with mother,' he said. 'I don't Adam and Eve it.'

George coughed.

'First the break-in at Tanya's shop. As I told you before, we identified the burglar and invited him down to the station for a chat. He claimed to be stealing to order and offered to repair the lock on the door "no harm done, gov". I told him he could reveal the name of the guy that hired him or spend a few years in the nick.'

'And?' I said.

'I had to keep him in a cell for twenty-four hours before he told me the truth. He said he had been hired by a man called John Smith.'

'That old chestnut,' said Gladys. 'That's definitely an alias. Honestly, how would anyone think they could fool the police with that name?'

'Um, well, he won't change his mind. He's adamant that the bloke who hired him was called John Smith. He even gave us his phone number, but of course it belonged to a burner phone.'

'How did he pay him?' I asked.

'Cash.'

'Naturally,' said Harry.

'Perhaps he doesn't have an account,' I said.

'What do you mean, Tan?' said George.

'An account in England. It may have been simpler to pay cash.'

'You mean he's not English? It's possible. Cash is also harder to trace.'

'What about fingerprints?' said Gladys. 'On the bank notes.'

'The burglar added the money to his stash in the bank and unfortunately, there is no way on earth we could identify the notes or the prints once he deposited it in his account. It would take forever to find notes with his prints on. They are probably circulating as we speak. And even if we did, the chances of identifying Mr Smith from prints found on those notes are infinitesimal.'

'At least we have a name. Even if it's a false one,' I said. 'Can you check if any know criminal uses that alias?'

'I think you should leave the policing to me. Why would anyone steal something from your shop?'

'They may have wanted the icon kept in Ryan's safe. It might be worth researching its background.'

'Why don't you use CCTV to identify him?' said Harry.

'We already did. That's how we caught the burglar.'

'I meant to use it to catch Smith, the man who hired him. If he paid in cash, they must have met somewhere to exchange the money. CCTV is ubiquitous these days. The exchange might be on film?'

'Brilliant,' I said.

'Honestly, who's the detective here?' said George. 'But it's a good idea. That's why Joe and the team are already searching. We're questioning the burglar again so we can establish the time, date and place of the handover. Right. Next on the agenda, Sophia's mobile phone.'

'Have you opened it?' said Gladys.

'Yes. And we downloaded the messages at last. It's got some really useful information on it.'

'Which is?' I said.

'Sophia received an anonymous text asking her if she knew Gladys Sabyani. She denied any knowledge of Gladys and told him she only knew one person with that surname, her father Sandor. But she thought the enquiry weird enough to text Sandor and ask him if he had a sister. Sandor told her he didn't have a sister, but he had married Gladys Fitch when he was very young, and that somewhere Sophia had an older sister. She was furious no one had told her about Joy and demanded to know where she lived. Sandor told her to try DNA testing.'

'She hadn't heard about me before?' said Gladys.

'Apparently not. Sandor told her he had looked for his daughter Joy earlier in life but come up blank. He didn't mention you at all. We think the man who texted Sophia found out where Sandor lived and tried to get information about Gladys from him by force. Poor Sandor only knew Gladys lived in Seacastle, but not that she was using her adopted parents' surname or that Joy lived down the road.'

'So Sophia inadvertently gave away Sandor's existence to the murderer? But how did the killer find Joy's pub?'

'I'm not sure. We think he may have followed Sophia to Seacastle and then killed her in a fit of rage,' said George.

'How dreadful,' said Gladys. 'So Joy is still in danger, but we don't know why.'

'You are too. I need you to come home where we can keep an eye on you.'

'But we haven't found Joy yet,' I said. 'And we are so close.'

'When is your return flight?'

'In two days' time.'

'Okay, but Harry, you need to keep a sharp eye out. The murderer may not be in England anymore. He may have found out that Joy didn't come home from Hungary.'

'I'll guard them with my life.'

'Let us know if CCTV captured an image of the man hiring the burglar. I think the two crimes are linked,' I said.

'Honestly, Jessica Fletcher will turn in her grave.'

Chapter 23

We locked the room again having straightened the bed covers and made sure it was pristine for the next guests. As we were leaving, my mobile phone vibrated again. Imre came on the line.

'Good morning,' he said. 'Would it be possible for you to bring Gladys to the bookshop? There is someone here I want you to meet.'

'We were just leaving. We'll be there shortly.'

I asked the others to wait for me while I collected a packet of Earl Grey tea from our room. It seemed like a polite gesture to give it to Imre since we had drunk so much of his coffee. I descended to the lobby and the three of us set out for the bookshop, leaving Magda frustrated in her quest for the latest news. The azure sky lifted our spirits as we walked the now familiar route. Gladys walked with a limp as if her hip hurt her, but she didn't complain. Her generation never does.

Imre welcomed us with a hug. Even Harry got included. He looked both embarrassed and pleased with himself. A young man with red hair watched the welcomes without moving from his chair. From the look of resentment he flashed at Imre, his presence was not entirely voluntary.

'This is Stefan. He works part time at the Jewish Archive with Katalin.'

'Not with her, exactly,' said Stefan. 'We don't speak much.'

'They were engaged to be married, but she found out he had, how do you say it? Played away,' said Imre, smirking.

'Ah, I know the feeling,' said Gladys.

'Me too,' I said.

'Anyway, because of their silent war, they have not been sharing some important pieces of information with each other.'

Imre nodded at Stefan who squirmed in his chair. 'Tell them what you told me.'

He sighed loudly before speaking, emphasising his reluctance to help us.

'A few weeks ago, a man came to the Archive inquiring about information relating to the Steinbergs. He told me his name was Janos Steinberg. He claimed to be the grandson of Erzsébet and Jozsef. He showed me his identification document. I had no reason to doubt him. He told me he was looking for his aunt Gladys who had been evacuated to England at the beginning of WWII. I brought out the box containing the belongings of Erzsébet Steinberg, but when he realised there was nothing of value in it, he lost interest. He commented on a list of objects he found inside the box but told me he already had a copy of the list. He wanted to know if anyone else had inquired about the family. I told him that the records showed no previous interest in the Steinbergs. He left, taking nothing except the details of the English family who adopted Gladys after the Steinbergs didn't survive the war. Days after his visit, Joy Wells turned up.'

'Did you tell her about Janos Steinberg?'

'I did. She seemed alarmed. She took the Steinberg box with her when she left.'

'What did Steinberg look like?' I asked.

'Late forties, Short, dark hair, deep blue eyes, oh, and he had a scar here.' He drew his finger down his cheek with his fingernail, leaving a white mark. 'I didn't like him. He seemed absent, somehow removed from normal life. I tried to tell him about his grandparents, but he didn't listen. I felt relieved when he left.'

'Why didn't you tell Katalin about him?'

'We're not talking. Since he took nothing with him. I didn't think it was important.'

'Not important? You may have got two people murdered,' said Harry.

Stefan deflated on the spot and became pale. I put my hand on Harry's arm and shook my head.

'Am I psychic?' asked Stefan. 'It's not my business if people want to kill each other over ancient history. Can I go now?'

He glanced at the door as if checking his escape route. Imre waited to see if anyone objected. When no-one did, he gave the youth a nod. Stefan stomped out without a backwards glance. We looked at each other in consternation.

'Pleasant young man,' said Gladys.

'The youth of today,' said Harry. 'He needs a few years of national service. That would soon sort him out.'

'Janos Steinberg and Jonas Kovacs could be the same person,' I said.

'You think my brother is involved in this somehow?' asked Gladys.

'It's more likely to be your nephew unless he's taken the elixir of youth. But what's he looking for?' said Harry. 'Whatever it is, it's not in the box. He won't be thrilled to discover his wife only took something from our car that he had already searched at the Archive.'

'He mentioned the Cooks' list again. You've never told us what happened to the items they brought over to England to back up your visa application. Might they contain the key to the mystery?'

'What do you mean?' said Gladys.

'Well, why would anyone want to harm you or your family? There must be something they want.'

Gladys sat blinking and scanning the past for a minute.

'After my visa had been arranged, someone delivered the items to the Fitches to keep for my parents. We didn't hear until years after the war that they had vanished. I still hoped they would turn up at our front door. A day never went by without the milkman, or the postman, or someone selling encyclopaedias ringing the doorbell and disappointing me. I was so convinced my parents would come and get me I told everyone at school about it. But time passed without a word from them and slowly I realised I was an orphan and would never leave the Fitches' house. One day Mrs Fitch took the box down from the attic and removed the valuables she could easily sell. She put them into an auction to pay for my upbringing. When I protested, she called me ungrateful and heartless. She stored the rest of the items back in the attic. I would sneak up to the loft sometimes and remove them. I remember a small plastic box with fake gemstones stuck on it and a painting of two men wearing what looked like bonnets.'

'Bonnets? How bizarre,' I said.

'Maybe that's why she didn't sell it,' said Gladys.

'What happened to them?'

'I have no idea. To tell you the truth, I forgot about the box as I got older. When Sandor came on the scene, I became infatuated with him. After moving in with him, I had a baby and got divorced in quick succession. The Fitches forced me to give her up for adoption. I ran away for good soon after, abandoning my past in the Fitches' house.'

'What happened to the remaining items?'

'I have no idea.'

'We'd better find out when we get home.'

'Are we going to leave without Joy?'

'Joy can look after herself now. She's bound to notice Boris isn't following her anymore.'

'Boris?' said Imre. 'Boris Peskov? That reprobate?'

'You know him?' I asked.

'Of course I do. He's a left over from the fringes of the Soviet Union. A nasty man who holds a grudge longer than the Irish.'

'He's been stalking her. We caught him at it, and I sent him away with a flea in his ear,' said Harry.

Imre threw his head back and guffawed.

'A flea? I don't recognise that expression. Very funny. I will make sure he doesn't bother her again. Believe me, I still have contacts in this game. I will tell Joy to go home and link up with you. I'm sure you'll solve this mystery together.'

'What about Janos Steinberg?' said Gladys.

'I'm pretty sure he's in England too,' I said.

'What's he doing there?' said Imre.

'I don't know, but it must be related to the list of items the Cooks brought back to England. We must find out where they are.'

'It's high time we went home,' said Harry.

Chapter 24

Despite being reluctant to leave Budapest, we persuaded Gladys to book a seat home on our flight to Gatwick. We invited Imre and Magda to dinner on our last night at the Felix to thank them for their help on our trip. Harry and I walked arm in arm, and Gladys followed behind with Magda. She had become visibly tired from the strain of her ordeal over the last few days. I admired her fortitude. It was difficult to comprehend how much sorrow she carried with her. No wonder she was crumpling under the weight of it all.

A full moon hung in the sky as we left the hotel, which became enveloped in a black cloud as we walked along. I felt a shiver run down my spine. Harry put his arm around me.

'I told you to wear a coat,' he said. 'Would you like my jacket?'

'No thank you, darling. I just had a moment.'

He raised an eyebrow at me, but receiving no clue, he shrugged.

'You're probably just hungry.'

Imre waited for us at the restaurant. He had oiled his hair so that the rebellious grey tufts had been subdued, and his head shone under the streetlamp.

'Ah, you're here. Fantastic. I love this place.'

Soon we were seated at a round table with full glasses of Hungarian red wine, which looked like fat rubies. The waitress brought menus in both languages to make ordering easier for us. Harry chose goulash again; on the pretext he couldn't order it in England. I didn't point out we could make it at home any time he fancied. Maybe goulash is like Guinness and tastes best in the country that invented it. I spent ages humming and hawing before choosing chicken Paprikash. Gladys ordered the same dish. Imre chose Rantott Hus, a sort of Schnitzel but using chicken instead of veal, and Magda the stuffed cabbage. We ate all the bread from the basket like a hoard of starving barbarians and the waitress brought us a new one.

'My mother always told me not to fill up on bread,' she said as she placed it on the table and grinned at us.

I recognised her as the same waitress who had served Harry and me on our first night out in Budapest. She had a tight t-shirt stretched over her baby bump and struggled to move through the tables. I watched as a woman put her hand out to feel the bump and I flinched for her. If anyone did that to me, they'd have earned a black eye. When I focussed back on our table, Imre was telling a complicated story about a lost dog he had returned to its owner. I noticed Gladys struggling to stay awake and Magda trying not to look bored. Harry chugged his wine and from the way his eyes were straying around the room, I guessed he felt it necessary to carry out surveillance on the room for mates of our pal Boris. Harry always amazed me with his ability to make everyone feel safe. I thanked the stars for sending me such a man.

The food arrived just as Imre arrived at his rather dull punchline and caused a lot more enthusiasm. He didn't seem to realise and tucked into his food with relish like the rest of us. The silence as we ate was a tribute to the quality of the meals. The delicious smells and vibrant colours of our meals increased our enjoyment. All around us, people made sounds of approval as they ate and drank. They say you eat more when others are eating with you. I had no problem polishing off my chicken and wiped the plate with some of the extra bread.

'Wow! You were hungry,' said Harry. 'You nearly beat me.' He leaned over and wiped a spot of sauce off my chin.

'It was yummy,' I said. 'We should make it at home. Mouse would love it.'

'I can't wait to go home,' said Gladys. 'I'm exhausted.'

'We all are. It's been an odd week.'

'Have you heard from Joy yet?' said Imre. 'I'm worried about her. My contact tells me Boris has slunk off to his hometown since his meeting with you, but she hasn't turned up.'

'Ryan told us she used to have a bolt hole underground. Does that ring a bell with you?' I asked.

'Underground? This city is full of limestone grottos and caves, but they are not inhabited. I'm not sure what he meant—'

My mobile phone rang at that precise moment. I picked it up to silence it and saw Ryan's name on the screen. I switched the speaker on the mobile phone to low volume and lifted my finger to my lips. Everyone leaned in to listen.

'Ryan? What's up?'

'Joy rang me. She's coming home.'

Gladys gasped and stuffed her napkin in her mouth her eyes shining. Imre shook his fist in the air in triumph and Magda burst into tears. I gathered myself to speak normally.

'Is she due at the pub?'

'No, she said she had to meet someone first. But I expect she'll be here in the next couple of days. When are you flying?'

'Our flight takes off at midday tomorrow.'

'Okay, I'll let you know as soon as she is in the country.'

'I'm so happy for you. I'll tell the others. We're all here at dinner.'

'Joy is in England?' said Gladys. 'Tell him not to tell her about me yet. I'll tell her myself.'

'She might already know,' said Harry.

'I haven't told her,' said Magda. 'If that's what you mean. We haven't spoken since she disappeared.'

'Me neither,' said Imre. 'Although no one told me it was a secret.'

'Okay. I've heard you all,' said Ryan. 'I promise not to tell her until you arrive. It'll be a shock for her, you know, having a mother after all these years.'

'It's worse for you,' said Harry. 'You've acquired a mother-in-law.'

This caused an explosion of laughter at our table. Imre looked around for the waitress.

'Champagne,' he said. 'We need champagne.'

Chapter 25

We were a motley crew who boarded the train to Seacastle after our flight home. Those of you over the age of thirty will be aware of the increasingly awful hangovers which afflict us over the passage of time. Flying with a hangover is possibly the worst thing you can do when your head is already hammering with dehydration and your stomach is threatening to eject the pain killers you swallowed with an ill-advised cup of coffee. Add to that the isolation from mutual suffering caused by an airline trying to make money by charging you to sit together, and the flight back from Budapest is one I would like to consign to the annals of history without a backward glance. I'm sure the woman beside me had good reasons to be proud of her grandchildren, but I didn't need to hear about every single one of them. Even groaning in misery didn't silence her on the subject.

'How are you feeling?' said Harry, grey-faced as we slid into our seats in the carriage.

'Grim,' I said.

'And you?' he asked Gladys.

'Oh, I'm excited. I can't wait to see Joy.'

'You have a constitution like an elephant,' I said.

'Oh no. I switched to sparkling water after one glass of wine. Old age brings the benefit of wisdom.'

I tried not to resent her cheerful demeanour. I doubted wisdom on matters of celebration would ever penetrate my thinking. But then she had every reason to feel cheerful, and I didn't want to be petty.

'Will you come with me to the Shanty if Joy has arrived?' said Gladys.

'We wouldn't miss it for the world,' said Harry, although I suspected he wanted to crawl into bed for a day or two and snuggle with me and Hades.

I ordered a taxi from the train and the driver waited outside the station for us. When we got home, Harry dealt with our bags, and I helped Gladys get hers out of the back. My mobile phone pinged, and I glanced at the screen. It showed an urgent message from Ryan asking me to call him as soon as I could. I held up my hand to Harry and Gladys and rang him.

'Ryan? What's up? Did Joy get home already?'

'Oh, Tanya! She's been kidnapped. Someone dropped a ransom note through the letterbox. Can you come with Harry and leave Gladys at home? This could be very distressing for her.'

I glanced at Gladys, hoping she hadn't heard. Her face turned a deathly white, and she dropped like a stone to the pavement. Harry broke her fall, so her head did not hit the ground, but she appeared to be unconscious.

'Ryan, Gladys has collapsed. We've got to take her to the hospital. Can you hang on until we can get her to safety? I'm truly sorry.'

'No, of course, I'm sorry too. I should have sent you a text.'

'She wouldn't have stayed at home. It's just as well she has collapsed here. Harry and I can put her in the Mini and drive her straight to the hospital without waiting for an ambulance.'

I hung up and stayed with Gladys while Harry paid the taxi and grabbed my car keys from inside the Grotty Hovel. Gladys did not wake up. Her eyelids fluttered but did not open. Harry picked her up as if she weighed no more than a loaf of bread. He laid her on her side on the back seat of the car and I slid in and placed her head on my lap. Then he drove to the hospital as fast as he could while keeping to the speed limit. I looked at her dear face and crossed my fingers she would be alright. Imagine finally finding your child after fifty years, and dying before you could tell her you loved her. I leant over and whispered in her ear.

'We're going to get your girl back. Your job is to get better. Don't you dare leave us, Gladys Fitch!'

Harry pulled up to the emergency entrance and picked Glady up again. I pushed the door open in front of them and he walked into the lobby where a nurse rushed up to us.

'What happened?' she asked.

'We don't know. She collapsed. She has been under immense emotional strain in the last couple of weeks.'

'That's helpful, thank you. I'll get her admitted straight away. Can you lie her on the stretcher in the passageway please?'

Harry followed the nurse through the secure doors, being careful not to hit Gladys's head. He came back a few minutes later to find me filling out the forms with any information I had. I was reminded of the last time I had been in this lobby with an American who tried to pay for treatment with his credit card.

'She says there's nothing we can do for now. I gave her my number and she'll let us know when to come back.'

'We have to leave her here alone?'

'Sweetheart, Gladys is unconscious. She's in the best hands possible. We should trust the doctors to deal with whatever is wrong with her. Ryan needs us, and he's marooned in his wheelchair with a ransom note. We have to go to him.'

I knew it made sense, but I felt as if I was betraying Gladys by leaving her there alone. What if she woke up alone? But then I imagined Ryan's distress, and I knew we had to go to the Shanty immediately.

We got back into the Mini and drove to the Shanty's car park. Harry stroked my cheek.

'Are you okay?' he asked.

'No. I'm not. But I'll manage.'

We left the car and walked along the narrow pathway to the pub. Seagulls whirled above our heads calling mournfully and I steeled myself for what was to come. When we arrived at the pub, Ryan had stuck a notice written with a felt-tip pen on the door announcing it would be closed until further notice. I pushed it open.

'Ryan, it's us,' said Harry.

His deep voice echoed through the pub. It felt emptier than a vacuum. Then the reassuring hum of Ryan's electric wheelchair broke the silence, and he motored into view from the back room. His drawn face lit up when he saw us.

'Oh, thank goodness you're here. I didn't know…' His voice petered out as it caught in his throat.

'Hang in there. We'll get her back. Do you have the note?' I said.

'It's right here,' he said, taking it out of the side pocket of his wheelchair and handing it to me.

I sat on the nearest chair and read the note. It had been written on a computer and printed on a piece of A4 paper. It read: *'I have your wife. You must hand over the painting from the Steinbergs' legacy or you won't see her alive again. I will contact you with the details in a few days. Do not speak to the police. If you do not comply, I will start sending you body parts to convince you of my intent.'*

I turned the piece of paper over, but it was blank. I handed it to Harry who read it with a furrowed brow.

'No phone number?' he said. 'How will they get in contact?'

'I'm not sure,' said Ryan. 'Joy has my number. They'll probably ask her to send any messages so their phones can't be traced. I already tried to call her, but her phone is off.'

'Do you know which painting he is referring to?' asked Harry.

'Who are the Steinbergs?. How can I find a random painting I've never heard of?'

'It's a long story, but we can explain much of it,' I said. 'Gladys's real surname is Steinberg.'

'And how is Gladys? It sounded serious,' said Ryan.

'We're not sure. The nurse promised to let us know when she wakes up.'

'And what about the police?' said Harry. 'We have to update George.'

'But you read the note. He'll mutilate my wife.'

'He doesn't know I and Harry are involved yet. We'll invite George to our house with Helen as a cover for handing George the ransom note. Joe Brennan has been looking into Sophia's phone record. Maybe they can conjure up a lead to this man's whereabouts.'

'But how will we find this painting?'

'We've got to start at the beginning with Gladys's adoptive parents, Mabel and Harold Fitch. Gladys told me she used to play with a painting in the loft. Perhaps it's still up there, covered in dust. You never know. I'll get Mouse to find out where they lived, because Gladys can't help us right now.'

'The painting this man wants used to be in Gladys's adoptive parents' loft?' said Ryan. 'I'm so lost.'

'Maybe we'd better make a pot of tea and tell you about our trip to Budapest?'

Despite his ferocious intelligence, Ryan found Gladys's complex family history hard to take in. He shook his head when we told him about our trip to Solymar to look for the Steinberg twins.

'I knew the communists took over after World War Two, but the repatriation of the ethnic Germans is new to me. How ironic poor Erzsébet's children were deported for being Bavarian, when they were in fact Hungarian Jews. The suffering never seems to end.'

'Only one twin survived to be deported, Janos. It seems he changed his surname to Kovacs, or his son did. I doubt Janos knew much about his actual mother,' said Harry.

'But he must have found out, or perhaps his son discovered the truth. Janos Steinberg had the most appalling luck. He could have emigrated to England with Gladys if he had been born earlier. Maybe jealousy destroyed him when he found out,' said Ryan.

'That's a brilliant suggestion. It would explain why his son, Janos, is out for revenge,' I said. 'He could have found out about Gladys's marriage and gone to question Sandor about the inheritance. Poor old Sandor had dementia. I doubt he ever knew about the items the Cooks brought to England. Maybe

Kovacs murdered him in a fit of pique when he couldn't get any sense out of him.'

'But what about Sandor's daughter Sophia? Why did he kill her? She had nothing to do with Gladys. They weren't even related.'

'But she looked just like Joy. What if he attacked her thinking she was Joy and killed her by mistake? He would have learned later he had killed the wrong woman.'

'He murdered two people for some worthless heirlooms? Why would he do that?' said Harry.

'Perhaps they're not worthless. He's asking for a painting in the ransom note. Presumably he saw it on the Cooks' list. Just because Gladys's adoptive mother Mabel thought the items she didn't sell were worthless, doesn't mean she got it right. Maybe she only sold the objects she thought were valuable, like the diamonds.'

'So the painting is still around? But how will we find it?' said Ryan.

'We can't ask Gladys until she wakes up. Why don't I ask Mouse to research the Fitches? He already told Gladys about the Cooks rescuing her from Budapest. I doubt it would be difficult for him to find their old house.'

'Gladys's house keys are in the Mini,' said Harry. 'I took them from her with her handbag in the hospital, just in case. She won't mind if we look in her house if it's necessary to save Joy. I remember where she kept her treasures. We could check for any clues to where the Fitches lived if Mouse doesn't come up trumps.'

'You're right. We can tell her as soon as she's awake. By then, hopefully we'll have good news. Time is of the essence. We simply can't waste a moment.'

'Keep me posted,' said Ryan. 'I'll man the phones and let you know if I hear anything.'

Chapter 26

George and Helen were delighted to be asked over to the Grotty Hovel for an Indian takeaway. Although Helen only lived two streets away, I didn't see her that often. I hadn't seen her at all since Sophia had been murdered outside the Shanty, which made me feel a little guilty. Having been married to George before they got together, with my blessing I might add, I knew how much being married to a police inspector could make someone into a grass widow. She tolerated his absences with good humour, but she suffered from loneliness with her daughter away at university. I could relate to that too with Mouse gone. I felt bad about deceiving them as to the point of their visit, but Joy's safety was paramount.

I sent Harry to buy the takeaway while I fed Hades and laid the table. Hades showed no interest in his expensive cat food and sat on the backrest of the sofa watching me put the red tablecloth on the dining table and lay the cutlery. The ratbag knew exactly what that meant. He had no scruples about sucking up to my guests for the choicest morsels. I expect I'd have done the same in his place. I lit some candles and switched the main light off, something I knew would irritate George no end, but I meant to fool anyone watching into believing we were having a nice social supper, and nothing to do with Joy Wells's disappearance.

The jar of chutney in the fridge was almost empty, but luckily I had bought a new one which sat in my store cupboard along with tins of spam I would never open and canned peaches I didn't even like, inherited from my parents who lived through the blitz and always kept supplies in case of nuclear war. Helen and I had divided the contents of their larder with as much care as their savings and other goods after they died in quick succession. I had bought Second Home with the proceeds and Helen had put hers in a savings account, which paid a pathetic rate of interest. I didn't know which of us acted more foolishly.

Harry burst in carrying the takeaway and looked around.

'They're not here yet? I thought I was late. I got talking to a lady whose mother's house I had cleared a few years ago. You know how it is.'

The smell of curry percolated through the room, and I shut my eyes to enjoy the aroma of the spices. I felt Harry's soft lips on mine and opened my eyes to find him gazing at me, his pupils enormous.

'Do we have to have dinner with George tonight? Can't we just leave the takeaway bag hanging on the front door with a message saying we have the plague?'

'This is about Joy, not dinner.'

'I know, but give me a snog before they get here, please?'

I squeaked as he deposited the bag on the table and swept me onto the sofa powerless to resist. Luckily, the doorbell rang at that moment, and I escaped from his arms, straightening my cardigan and blushing furiously.

'I'm never talking to anyone at the takeaway ever again,' said Harry.

I shrugged at him and opened the door. Helen entered first, arms open for a hug. George followed her, looking tired and plump. He always ate more when he was overworked. KitKats formed a major part of his diet when he needed constant boosts of energy to work long days. Harry shook his hand and gave Helen a tight squeeze, which made her pink with pleasure. I kissed them both hello and poured them a glass of wine each. We removed the food from the bag and served ourselves. I wanted to wait until George had eaten before giving him the ransom note, but he picked up on my tense mood after I sighed loudly without thinking as I helped myself to rice.

'Okay, spit it out,' he said. 'You're not fooling anyone.'

'She fooled me,' said Helen.

'You don't know her like I do,' said George, which caused a roar of protest from Helen and a guffaw from Harry.

'Somebody has kidnapped Joy Wells,' I said.

George dropped his fork on his plate and a blob of curry flew up onto his shirt. Helen rolled her eyes and tried to wipe it off with her napkin, making it worse.

'Leave it, leave it,' said George. 'We'll have to inform Interpol immediately.' He patted his pockets for his mobile phone.

'You don't understand. She's in England. We think the man who murdered Sophia and Sandor Forrest has taken her prisoner. Ryan received a ransom note demanding a painting that belonged to Joy's grandmother.'

'Why is everything so complicated in Seacastle? What about a nice breaking and entering, or a common assault?'

'Murder is pretty straightforward,' said Harry.

George shook his head.

'Is the painting at the Shanty?'

'Nobody knows where it is. It came here as part of a consignment from Hungary to form the basis of a visa application for Gladys Fitch,' I said.

'Gladys? No wonder she followed you to Hungary. I should have guessed something dodgy was happening.'

'Gladys is a Hungarian Jew who was sent to England before World War II. In order to get a visa, she had to have enough finance to pay her keep. Her mother sent a box of family heirlooms over with the Cook sisters. We think the painting formed part of the belongings.'

'Oo, I know who the Cook sisters are,' said Helen. 'Remember, treasure? We saw an item on the BBC news.'

'The opera mad old bats?'

'You mean the incredibly brave women of conscience, don't you?' said Harry, drawing his eyebrows together.

'Yes, sorry, that was uncalled for. They're not the ones getting involved in things that don't concern them.'

'Actually, they were—'

George cut me off. 'Do you have the ransom note?'

I handed it to him in a Ziplock bag.

'It will have my fingerprints on it,' I said.

'That doesn't surprise me,' said George. 'Why all the cloak and dagger? Couldn't you have brought this to the station?'

He read the note through the plastic. 'Oh. I get it. The kidnapper mustn't know the police are involved.'

'Exactly.'

'Did your research in Budapest identity this man?'

'We think his name is Jonas Schmidt,' said Harry. 'He's Gladys's long-lost nephew. His father was Gladys's brother.'

George raised an eyebrow.

'Has she contaminated you too?' he asked. 'Honestly, Tan, you're incorrigible pulling Harry into this investigation with you. You should know better.'

'I'm sorry, but it's not like I had a choice.'

George sighed.

'What's our next move?'

'While your lot search for Schmidt, we'll find the painting,' I said. 'Just in case Ryan needs to set up a handover.'

'No handover, I forbid it. It's in police hands now. We'll locate the artwork.'

'Be reasonable. The painting's an antique. I have contacts in the trade. Harry can use his job as a house clearer to ask questions. We can probably find the painting quicker than you, arousing fewer suspicions with the kidnapper. I'll ask Mouse to track down the house where Gladys lived as a child, and we'll work from there.'

'What will you do with the painting?' said George.

'You need cheese to bait a mouse trap,' said Helen.

'My thoughts exactly,' I said.

'Don't you dare,' said George. 'Promise me you won't do anything without informing me first. If this man has already murdered two people, he won't hesitate to kill again.'

'I promise.'

Chapter 27

When I told Mouse about Gladys being in the hospital, he came straight home on the next train. I tried to get him to stay in Portsmouth, but his holidays had started, and nothing could keep him away once he knew we needed him. It's not as if I tried that hard to dissuade him from coming. We all missed Mouse, and he had a sixth sense for computer searches. Nobody could track down something on the net quicker than him. While I waited for him to arrive, I called Ryan and updated him on our dinner with George. Ryan had not heard anything from Joy's kidnapper.

'It would help if we knew what he looked like,' he said.

'We think he's short with dark hair and deep blue eyes, but that doesn't exactly make him stand out,' I said. 'It's a pity you don't have CCTV in the car park.'

Then I remembered.

'Sorry, I've got to go. I need to call someone urgently,' I said. 'It could be important.'

'Will you let me know?'

'Of course.'

DI Antrim answered straight away.

'Hi there, Miz Bowe. How can I assist you today?' he said.

'Did you ever get CCTV of the man who murdered your pensioner at Hove?'

'I'm not sure. We've been snowed under with illegal immigrant gangs for weeks. The pleasant weather has encouraged them to flood the channel with small boats.'

'We think your murderer killed Sophia Forrest.'

'The poor woman who was murdered outside the Shanty? What on earth links the two murders?'

'Sophia was the daughter of Sandor, but her resemblance to Joy Wells got her killed.'

'Joy Wells who runs the pub?'

'Yes, Sophia was her half-sister.'

'Sandor was Joy Wells's father?'

'Yes.'

'And the murderer?'

'We think he's a man called Jonas Kovacs or Janos Steinberg. He's the nephew of Gladys Fitch, Joy's mother.'

'My head is spinning now. Is George in the loop?'

'Of course. I'm hoping the CCTV may have picked up an image of your murderer, we can use to identify him.'

'Can this wait? We must capture this gang before they flee the country. We revise the CCTV tomorrow.'

'Not really. Joy Wells has been kidnapped, and we think the murderer is responsible.'

'Why didn't you say so? I'll get on it straight away and send any results directly to George. It shouldn't take us long. We already have the footage, the date, and the approximate time of death.'

'Thanks Terry.'

'You owe me a beer.'

'I owe you many.'

Mouse came through the front door as I hung up the call, and I leapt up to hug him. I found it hard to let go.

'Honestly Mum, you'd think I'd been away for ten years.'

'It feels like you have.'

'What's all this I hear about Gladys and Joy?'

'Would you like a sandwich? I'll make one and tell you the whole saga.'

Mouse's eyes opened wider and wider as I recounted the story from start to finish, his sandwich forgotten on his plate. When I finished, he took a huge bite.

'We've got to find the painting,' he said. 'Give me a minute to scarf this down and I'll get on my computer.'

The cat flap whacked against the door and a large black purring machine leapt up on the table, shoving his face into Mouse's, making a noise like an electric mower. Mouse tolerated this display of love for a good five minutes before reaching for his laptop. Hades did not appreciate being usurped and tried to sit on the keyboard. Mouse stuffed Hades into his jacket and raised the zip, so only Hades's nose poked out. He typed instructions into his browser at light speed. I had developed a pretty steady eighty words per minute as a journalist, but Mouse typed so fast I could hardly see his fingers. He screwed up his eyes and his nose twitched like Samantha on Bewitched. Then he was off again, metaphorical steam rising from his keyboard.

While he muttered and searched, I folded the laundry and procrastinated. I needed to appear at the shop where Ghita and Roz had been in charge for days. I hoped the new stock we had left there before going to Budapest had made it worth our while, but I hadn't called to check on them. They understood that once I got embroiled in a mystery, I often disappeared for days. They tolerated these absences on the unspoken agreement I would spill the beans when I reappeared. A grunt of satisfaction told me Mouse had unearthed something.

'Check this out,' he said, spinning the screen around.

He had found the address of the last known address of Mabel and Horace Fitch, a terrace house in Shoreham, not twenty minutes away and looked it up on Great Move. The house had been purchased over thirty years before. The present owner was an Elsie Riley. I decided to go directly there without waiting for Harry, even though he was due back from Sainsbury's soon. I couldn't afford to delay.

'Do you fancy a spin out to Shoreham?'

'Is that a real question?'

Harry had taken the Mini to the supermarket, so we jumped into the van. Mouse sighed as he pushed the cassettes to one side and plugged in his phone.

'Honestly, the Ark probably had a cassette player too. I don't understand why you don't use streaming.'

'You wait. One day a huge solar flare will knock out all the satellites and Harry and I will be the only people left on earth with music in our vehicle.'

'Anarchy will reign if the satellites fail. No electricity or banking systems, no phones, no internet. Playing music on a cassette will be the least of your worries.'

'Meanwhile, can you put in the Joni Mitchell please? I fancy something soothing.'

Mouse shoved the cassette into the player and turned up the volume. Even though he complained about it, he loved our music. I watched as his face relaxed and he sang along with me. When we got to our destination, we let the song finish.

'I'll do the talking,' I said.

'As if I'd dare,' said Mouse.

I knocked on the door, and a young woman opened it, blinking in the midday sunlight.

'Can I help you?' she said to Mouse, ignoring me completely.

Mouse smirked.

'Yes, my name is Andrew Carter. My great grandparents used to live in this house. I'm doing a project at university on my family tree. It's possible some family papers may have been forgotten in the attic many years ago. I wonder if you might let me search up there?'

'The attic? Oh, no, I don't think so. I'm only renting this house. The owner might not like it.'

Mouse pouted and tossed his black curls.

'She wouldn't know,' he said. 'I promise not to tell anyone, only I'm close to failing the year. This would save me.'

He gave her a pleading glance from under his long lashes. She bit her lip and blushed crimson.

'I'm not sure,' she said.

'Please. I promise not to make a mess. I'll only take a few minutes to check under the eaves.'

She sighed.

'Okay, but only you. She stays outside,' she said, pointing at me.

What a cheek!

'I was hoping you'd say that,' said Mouse, following her inside.

She glanced at me in triumph, and I pretended to be disappointed, letting my shoulders sag as I walked back to the car. I made sure she didn't see me pump my fist.

The sun had come out and a pair of chaffinches squabbled in a plum tree in next door's front garden. I watched their antics for a few minutes before I realised I too was being observed. A plump woman in an ancient Laura Ashley dress and a pink cardigan stood in the house's doorway a cigarette hanging from her mouth.

'Good morning,' I said. 'Lovely day, isn't it?'

'I know you,' she said, pointing her finger at me. 'You're that lady what's got the junk shop in Seacastle.'

'Yes, that's right. I'm Tanya Bowe.'

'You'll be looking for Elsie then.'

'Elsie?'

'Her what did the car boot sales at Shoreham Airport? She doesn't live here no more. They moved her to a care home when her niece arrived. I knew it, I did. As soon as I saw that hussy move in.'

'You knew what?'

'She'd got her beady eyes on Elsie's house. She weren't here six months before she shipped Elsie off to a home and emptied the house of her belongings. It's a rental now.'

'That's awful. I bet Elsie had some nice old pieces of furniture in her house.'

'Oh, you know. Most of it were junk, like the stuff you sell.'

I restrained myself from punching her in the nose.

'Do you know what happened to Elsie's junk? I might be interested in buying some of it.'

She narrowed her eyes and lit a cigarette, blowing smoke rings into the air.

'Would you now? Well, if you've got a tenner, I've got her niece's telephone number. She told me Elsie's stuff is in storage, waiting for her to die.'

'In storage?'

'Like I said. I think there's a nephew who wanted to see it before Gemma got rid of it. That's her name, Gemma. So, do you want that number then?'

When Mouse emerged empty-handed half an hour later, covered in dust and cobwebs, I had already phoned Gemma, who had been ecstatic at the thought of offloading some of her aunt's junk. That word again. Had none of them heard of Antique's Road Show? She had agreed to meet me at the storage depot in Seacastle in an hour. I let Mouse suffer for a few moments before I told him about the storage unit.

'Seriously,' he said. 'Are you hoping she kept it? How will we identify it?'

'It's the only lead we have. Investigation is mostly about dead ends. It only takes one lucky find to break a case.'

'You sound like Dad.'

'I hate to admit it, but your father is right.'

We pulled into the storage depot and looked around. Gemma had described herself as blonde and glamorous. I spotted a woman in a sprayed-on faux leopard-skin catsuit with black patent leather boots and a platinum wig.

'That'll be her,' I said.

'Wow! That's some outfit,' said Mouse.

We walked over to her, and she proffered her hand to Mouse.

'Enchanté,' she said. 'I'm Gemma.'

'My son, Mouse,' I said. 'And I'm Tanya.'

'Nice to meet you both. Well, don't just stand there gawping. I haven't got all day.'

She led us over to a rusty container and handed me the key, staring at my hands with undisguised contempt.

'Can you do the honours, dearie? I don't want to risk my manicure.'

I took the key and opened the door to an Aladdin's cave of nineteen-fifties kitsch. I could hardly contain my excitement.

'Dreadful old tat isn't it,' said Gemma. 'Living in a time warp, our Elsie. I swear she hasn't bought anything since the sixties..'

'I understand Elsie's nephew wanted some of her stuff,' I said.

'Oh no. He took one look and washed his hands of it. I intended to pay someone to remove the lot.'

I casually picked up a wonderful, coloured bread bin which was perching on a gorgeous painted kitchen cabinet.

'I can understand that, but I might salvage a few items for my shop. How about I take the lot and save you paying to have it removed? I'll keep a few bits and junk the rest.'

Suspicion registered on her face.

'You'll take the lot? Really? What's in it for you?'

'As I told you, there may be some objects I can sell, and my partner has a clearance van, so he'll take the rest. We do this all the time.'

'Honestly, Mum,' said Mouse. 'Not more junk. Let her deal with it.'

Gemma rubbed her chin.

'This storage unit costs me a bloody fortune every month. If you can clear it today, you can have the lot.'

'It's a deal.'

'I'll cancel the unit. I doubt they'll give me a refund, but you never know. You'd better clear everything, mind you.'

'We'll sweep the floor as well,' I said.

When she had swaggered off, wiggling her bottom at Mouse, I took out my phone and called Harry.

'Have you finished the shopping?' I asked.

'Yes, but where are you? Has Mouse arrived yet?'

'I'll tell you all about it if you come to the storage depot.'

'How mysterious. I'll be with you shortly.'

Chapter 28

I couldn't disguise my excitement on the phone and Harry arrived in a state of anticipation. He parked the Mini and came over to us, rubbing his hands together. He whistled in amazement as he took in the contents of the container.

'Blimey! This looks promising,' he said. 'Did these items come from the Fitch's house?'

'The woman who bought the house from them lived her whole life there. She used to be a dealer at Shoreham car boot sale, so I often met her there without realising any of this. She must have kept all the best pieces for her house. And now nobody wants them.'

'We do,' said Harry. 'It's our lucky day. Let's empty this treasure trove into the van.'

'Remember the painting depicts two men with bonnets on.'

'Bonnets?' said Mouse. 'what sort of bonnets?'

'I don't know. Gladys used to play with this painting when she was a little girl. She told me she remembered them having a weird sort of bonnet on.'

We worked our way through the container, sorting the pieces which I could sell in my shop straight into the van and putting the rest to one side for Harry to collect on his second visit to the depot. I noticed Harry give Mouse an affectionate hug around his shoulders. That boy had us both in his thrall. I couldn't get over the quality of some articles we were loading into the van. The shop would leap in class when I added them to the stock.

'Hey, look at these!' said Mouse. 'We've struck gold.'

He had checked the contents of a cardboard box and found a stack of large ledgers. He handed one to me and I opened it on the bonnet of the Mini. The ledger contained line after line of purchases and sales over a period of many years. Eureka!

'They are. Elsie seems to have kept a record of every single item she bought and sold over the last thirty years. It's quite extraordinary. She even lists the client's name for every piece. If she sold that painting, we'll find it here and discover who bought it.'

'You'd better take them to the shop then,' said Harry. 'I suspect we're talking overtime for Roz and Ghita.'

I placed the box into the van with the other stock, and we were done soon afterwards. We left Mouse to guard the container's remaining contents and drove to Second Home jubilant with our haul. I followed Harry in the Mini to avoid stranding it at the depot. We left it parked outside the Grotty Hovel and then I jumped into the van for the quick trip to Second Home. I texted Roz that we were on our way and she waited outside with Ghita and a trolley I had acquired from Grace who had upgraded to a new one. We unloaded the boxes as fast as we could and stored them in the back room of the shop. I had my fingers crossed not to attract the interest of a passing traffic warden until we had finished. Harry drove off as soon as the van was emptied and returned to the depot to reload the van with the remaining furniture and goods. Roz and Ghita helped me to bring the larger pieces which had remained on the pavement inside, piling everything haphazardly in the shop. One lovely Art Deco chest of drawers didn't even enter the place, as a dealer friend of mine was passing in his van and made me an offer I couldn't refuse. I shoved the notes he paid me into the cash register and gave the girls a hug.

'Sorry to leave you in the lurch. I promise to update you on every detail of our trip to Budapest, but first I have a massive favour to ask you.'

'What sort of favour?' said Roz.

I took one ledger out of its box and handed it to her.

'How can we help?' said Ghita.

'We're looking for a painting of two men, possibly wearing weird bonnets. We need to find out who bought it and where they live if possible.'

'Weird bonnets? Seriously?' said Roz. 'There must be twenty-five Ledgers here.'

'Harry and Mouse will come and help us as soon as they leave the van at the house. It's really important. I can't tell you why yet, but it's a matter of life or death.'

'My favourite,' said Roz. 'Deadly jeopardy can't be beaten as a motive to search for clues.'

'We can fuel ourselves with the cake I made with my new recipe,' said Ghita.

'Let's take the ledgers upstairs to the Vintage. What flavour is your cake?'

'Rhubarb and Orange. I tried it earlier. I think it's one of my best ever.'

'It sounds revolting,' said Roz.

'You don't have to eat it,' said Ghita.

'I'm starving and I think it sounds lush,' I said, herding Ghita upstairs. 'Who wants coffee?'

'A cappuccino for me,' said Roz. 'I'm struggling to stay awake after a spot of night fishing with Ed.'

'I've never heard it called that before,' said Ghita. 'I'll have a tea, please.'

Ghita's cake tasted like summer and garden parties. The sponge had just enough juice soaked through to make it fruity.

'Not bad,' said Roz, licking her fingers. 'It needs a spoonful of whipped cream on top.'

'Is that what Ed said last night?' said Ghita.

'Okay, you two. Let's get started on these ledgers,' I said. 'Make a note of the date on which any painting was sold. I often bought stuff from Elsie's stall, and I don't remember seeing paintings on it.'

We took a ledger each and worked our way systematically through the pages, ignoring all the entries except those containing the word painting. It was painstaking work and soon the words swam before my eyes in Elsie's spidery writing. When Harry and Mouse arrived, they raved about Ghita's cake and had a coffee each before settling down to the tedious job of revising the ledgers. Even with five of us checking the entries, it still took hours to go through every ledger. In the end, we only found references to sixty paintings, none of which had a description matching two men in bonnets or any other sort of hats. Most of the pieces of art were still lifes, matching the preference of amateur artists.

'I wish she'd wake up,' I said. 'Maybe she'd remember something else about the painting that would help us identify it.'

'You wish who would wake up?' said Ghita.

'Oh! Haven't I said? Gladys is in hospital.. She had a turn outside our house when we got back from Budapest.'

'In hospital? That's terrible. Will she be okay?'

'Gladys went with you?' asked Roz. 'I didn't know that.'

'She followed them later,' said Mouse. 'Is she going to be okay?'

'The doctors think so, but she's at the heart of this mystery. Maybe we'd all better have another coffee, then Harry and I will tell you the complete story.'

I couldn't tell which was more shocking for our friends. The fact Joy worked for MI6 or that Gladys had been smuggled out of Hungary as a baby to avoid the Nazis. Mouse, who had been kept in the loop for some of the story, couldn't believe our encounter with Boris or the sad story of Gladys's parents. Roz and Ghita were more amazed by the link between Gladys and Joy.

'Truth is stranger than fiction,' said Roz. 'I would've found this far-fetched if it happened in a novel, but Gladys always struck me as someone keeping secrets.'

'It's not like we didn't have our suspicions about Ryan and Joy though,' said Ghita. 'All those trips to Eastern Europe.'

'Can we visit Gladys in the hospital?' asked Mouse. 'I thought she would tell Joy about being her mother straight away. I can't believe it's still a secret.'

'I don't think I can cope with so many secrets at once,' said Roz. 'I might burst.'

'You'll have to risk it,' I said. 'All of this is confidential for now. We must save Joy from the clutches of this madman.'

'But how can we help?' said Ghita, a tremor in her voice. 'We can't find the stupid painting and dear Joy is in danger.'

'George and the team are following this man's trail. We should keep the story to ourselves and support Gladys and Ryan where possible,' said Harry. 'We all have to keep quiet until then.'

Chapter 29

We packed the ledgers away in their box and shut up shop for the evening. Exhausted by the stress of the search, I didn't feel like cooking, so we bought a Chinese takeaway from Mr Chen on our way home. The sweet smell of the plum sauce permeated the car and made us drool with hunger. Mouse passed around the prawn crackers to keep us from fainting with hunger. We parked in the street parallel to ours and walked to our door carrying the bags of takeaway Chinese goodies. I noticed two familiar figures coming towards us as we neared the house. George and Joe came into focus under the streetlamps as they approached us, trying to appear nonchalant.

I ushered them indoors, checking the street for any sign we were being observed. All the talk of street craft in Budapest had made me nervous. I felt a little foolish scanning the streets, but I did it anyway. Only Betty Staples from across the road opened her door for a quick peep and quickly closed it again when George gave her one of his 'police business' looks. He's not as imposing as Harry, but he can intimidate most people if he puts his mind to it. We filed inside and sat around the dining table. As usual, we had enough food to feed a platoon, so there was plenty for George and Joe too. We laid out the containers of sweet and sour pork, beef noodles, ingredients for duck pancakes, fried rice and brown rice and chicken chow mein. I took the soy sauce and the plates and cutlery from the kitchen and Harry opened a few beers from his stash. Usually, I don't drink beer, but for some reason it went down a treat.

George and Joe watched us set up the meal with increasing impatience. Once we were ready to eat, they fell on the food like ravenous wolves, without looking up or pausing for breath. I recognised the signs and gave them a chance to calm their hunger before filling us in on the news. Finally, George burped and leaned back, signifying satiety. Joe dug him in the ribs with a look of disapproval.

'Honestly Dad,' said Mouse.

'Sorry. I shouldn't have eaten so fast, but Joe and I didn't have time for lunch.'

'We've eaten all your food,' said Joe. 'Shall I order some more?'

'We always buy way too much,' said Harry. 'You've saved us from eating chow mein for breakfast.'

'I like chow mein for breakfast,' said Mouse.

I rolled my eyes at him, and he shut up.

'The good news is that we have identified the murderer thanks to Terry Antrim,' said George.

'DI Antrim? How's he involved?' asked Harry, bristling.

George was not famous for his tact, but for once, he poured oil on stormy waters. 'Terry sent me CCTV images from the murder of a pensioner in a care home in Brighton. The murdered man was Sandor Sabyani, but he used his second wife's surname, Forrest.'

'Sophia's father? But wasn't he also married to Gladys?' said Mouse.

'He was Joy's father,' I said.

'Crikey,' said Harry. 'I hadn't tied all the threads together.'

'Did you recognise the person in the images?' I asked.

'We didn't, but Nick Styles did,' said Joe.

'Your burglar,' said George. 'The man who broke into Second Home.'

'Are they partners in crime?' said Mouse.

'You could say that,' said Joe. 'We called Nick in to ask him about the man that hired him. We were trying to establish when and where he got paid to rob Second Home. We were hoping to get CCTV from the place they used, but Nick spotted a still image from the care home murder on my computer screen and he asked me why I was wasting his time asking about our meeting when I already had an image of the man who hired him. It took me a few seconds to realise he was talking about the man on the screen.'

'John Smith is the murderer?' I said.

'I'll bet you a million quid his real name is Jonas Kovacs,' said Harry.

'Hang on,' said Mouse, tapping furiously on his tablet.

'What's up?' I said.

'Yes!' said Mouse, pumping his fist. 'Kovacs is Hungarian for Smith. And Janos is John.'

'Janos Kovacs? Gladys's nephew?' asked Harry.

'Also known as Jonas Schmidt,' I said.

'But why is he desperate for the painting?' said George.

'It must be valuable, or at least he must believe it is,' I said. 'Enough to threaten Joy's life.'

'Even with a photo, I'm not sure we can track him down in time,' said Joe.

'Do you want me to talk to Jim Swift of the Seacastle Echo? He could publish a photograph of Kovacs in the paper?' I said.

'Too dangerous,' said George. 'Remember the police are not supposed to be involved. We'll put a BOLO out to the local forces, to alert us if they see him but not to approach unless Joy is in danger.'

'Have you had any luck locating the painting?' asked Joe.

'Not yet,' I said. 'We thought we had something, but it was a dead end. I'm waiting for Gladys to wake up and give us better details of the painting to narrow down the search.'

'Time is short. Luckily, there is only one route into the Shanty and one out. If we can spot him going there, we can trap him.'

'So why do you need the painting?' asked Harry.

'What do you mean?' said Joe.

'If you can set up an ambush for this geezer, you don't need the painting. Ryan can tell Kovacs to come and get it, and you can rush the pub once he is inside.'

'Won't Ryan be at risk?' I said. 'He's at a disadvantage in his chair.'

'Don't kid yourself,' said George. 'Joy has a licence to carry since they tried to assassinate her. I'm sure she didn't take the gun to Budapest with her to look for her parents.'

'A licence to kill? Like James Bond?' said Mouse.

George sighed.

'Something like that. Joy is notorious in post-Cold War Eastern Europe. Ryan got shot protecting her. MI6 told the Super that she's still a target.'

'It still sounds risky. What if he refuses to tell us where Joy is being held?'

'Let's see what the murderer will demand when he speaks to Ryan. He's unlikely to leave it long. He may get his ducks in a row first so he can flee the country again without being captured.'

'That's if it's Kovacs acting alone,' I said.

'I've got a bad feeling about this,' said Harry. 'I should have dealt with that guy Peskov while I had the chance.'

'Who the hell's Peskov?' said George.

'No one important,' I said. 'Harry's confused.'

I sneaked in a glance, which told him I didn't believe that. He nodded. Joe Brennan put down his stylus with a sigh.

'I'm not surprised,' he said. 'Slow Horses isn't half as complicated as this.'

'My favourite show,' said Mouse. 'But I don't understand any of it.'

'We should watch it,' I said. 'I love Gary Oldman.'

After George and Joe left, Harry did the washing up while I dictated everything I could remember about the case to Mouse. He posted it into ChatGPT and asked them for ideas about how to stop the kidnapper. Unfortunately, at the first mention of murder, the algorithm shut down and refused to help us. Mouse shook his head.

'Tiktok's the same. You have to say unalive for kill or murder, and spice for sex or they ban your post.'

'Seriously? What's that about?' I asked.

'Oh, all the underage users.'

'Should I be shocked or pleased?'

'It's kind of contradictory. I guess they're worried about using ChatGPT to plan murders or something.'

'It won't stop AI from taking over the world, you know. We are all doomed.'

'Don't be silly, Mum.'

'I suppose I'll have to solve it myself, then.'

'Weren't you always going to ignore Dad's advice?'

'That's fair. Come and give Hades and me a cuddle.'

Chapter 30

Despite the risks involved, George set up a trap to capture Jonas Kovacs at the Shanty. Joe planned out a perimeter set back two hundred metres from the car park where he would station his units. No one approaching the pub would spot them, but a single keystroke from Ryan would alert them to the arrival of Kovacs at the Shanty and they could move in and seal off his escape routes. Ryan's CCTV cameras placed on vantage points on the roof through which he could see people approaching from any direction, gave them the advantage they needed to spot Kovacs making his approach to the pub. Ryan told George he had installed them to keep Joy safe, but he had never expected to use them to catch her kidnapper.

Harry had forbidden me from getting involved in the operation, and to tell the truth, I agreed with him. George and his men, and the reinforcements from the armed police, were highly trained. I brought Mouse with me to Second Home where I could keep an eye on him too. He did not take kindly to this.

'What about my cyber skills?' he said. 'Most policemen are still living in the stone age. They might need me.'

'Your father would never forgive me if I put you in the line of fire. When Kovacs finds out Ryan doesn't have the painting, he may lose control.'

But I worried about Ryan too, stuck on his own in a wheelchair. I crossed my fingers he had as many gadgets as Bond's Q to keep him safe. I rang him in the morning for an update, but he hadn't heard from Kovacs yet. I didn't stay on the line in case Kovacs called at the same time. Ryan sounded stressed and tired. Hardly surprising, as he can't have been getting much sleep.

My mobile phone vibrated on the shop counter, and I picked it up to see a number I didn't recognise. I almost cut them off, but I answered in case it was important.

'Hello?'

'Is that Tanya Bowe?'

'Yes.'

'I'm Gillian, the duty nurse on Gladys Fitch's ward at Seacastle Hospital. I thought you should know Gladys has woken up. She's not talking yet, but she might enjoy seeing you anyway.'

'Thank you so much. I'll be right there.'

I found Mouse glued to his screen as usual doomscrolling. I tapped him on the shoulder, making him jump.

'Let's go. Gladys is awake.'

'Shouldn't we wait here?'

'What for? Your father doesn't want us interfering with the police operation. He said nothing about seeing Gladys.'

Minutes later, we were in the Mini, crawling through town to the hospital. As usual, every traffic light turned red as we approached, adding to my stress.

We parked as near to the entrance as we could and ran inside.

'Where's the fire?' asked the receptionist.

She sent us upstairs to a quiet sunny ward where Gladys lay in a bed at the far end. The only other occupant snored like a bulldozer pushing earth up a road. A nurse followed us into the ward.

'Hi. Are you Tanya? I'm Gillian. Gladys seems to be asleep, but if you would like to sit with her for a while and chat, she may come round again.'

'Thank you, we will.'

Mouse sat on one side of the bed, and I sat on the other, holding her hands and telling her about Ghita's cakes and George's moods. She lay serene and fragile with her grey hair spread over the pillow like an elderly princess. Then I changed the subject to the objects brought to England by the Cooks and asked her if she remembered anything about the painting. Her eyes flickered for a moment but stayed closed. I told her how important it might be to find it soon.

'What colour bonnets were the men wearing?' said Mouse.

Gladys appeared to laugh in her sleep.

'You told me about them,' I said. 'What colour were they?'

Gladys muttered something, but I didn't catch it. I leaned forward.

'Say it again.'

'Not bonnets.'

She giggled.

'Silly girl. Not bonnets. See.'

She released her hand from mine and lifted it off the bed covers with great effort. Her arm wavered in the air and her finger emerged and pointed at the opposite wall of the ward at a painting of the Virgin

Mary with her baby Jesus. For a moment, I didn't understand what she meant.

'Haloes?'

Her hand dropped to the cover.

'A picture of a saint?' said Mouse. 'I don't remember any of those in the ledgers.'

I felt my heart skip a beat.

'Icon. She means an icon.'

'We must have missed it on the list. We were so concentrated on finding a painting.'

'But I bought an icon from Elsie Dwyer. It's the one I had in the shop. I bought it with several other bits and bobs in a box. I gave Roz a Bakelite art deco jewel box from it.'

'Where is the icon now?'

'Ryan has it. He took it to give to Joy on her birthday, at the party where Kovacs murdered Sophia Forrest.'

'Call him.'

I took out my phone and dialled Ryan's number, but the call didn't go through. I tried again without success. Mouse tried too, but Ryan's phone didn't pick up the call.

'He needs to know about the icon,' said Mouse. 'If he hands it over, Joy will be safe.'

'But we can't enter the Shanty. George's boys are monitoring the area, and they'll spot us going in. We could wreck the operation.'

'Who said we were entering via the car park?'

I blinked at him.

'And what do you mean by that? Are we going to parachute in?'

'Honestly, grown-ups don't know everything. There's a path up the bluff at the back of the Shanty we used to climb when we were at school. Shaylah sold us cans of cider on the sly. Ryan and Joy never found out.'

'I suspect they did. Is it still there?'

'The path? Oh yes. A new generation of schoolboys are using it to get contraband booze. Shaylah makes a fortune. She buys beer and cider at the cash-and-carry and sells it from the back of the Shanty. She charges a percentage on top.'

I laughed.

'It wasn't there in my day. We used to get our older siblings to buy cans for us in the supermarket, although Helen always refused. She was such a goody two shoes. Is the path steep?'

'I couldn't get up there in those,' he said, pointing at my pixie boots. 'But you might.'

'Let's go.'

Following Mouse's directions, we arrived at the bottom of the bluff on which the Shanty stood with its wonderful view of Pirate's Harbour. I had never ventured down the minor road before. Its deep potholes and gravelly surface made the Mini grumble in rebellion.

'Stop here,' said Mouse.

I stared upward and spotted a narrow path without a guardrail which headed away from the Shanty and then switched back on itself. My stomach flipped at the thought of climbing it, but we had no choice. If Ryan knew he had the icon, he stood a chance of getting Kovacs to reciprocate without the risk of violence. It was especially important if Ryan couldn't signal the police because of his faulty reception.

'Come on,' I said. 'You go first. You know the path and if I fall I won't take you with me.'

The first few steps were the worst. The rock path had crumbled because of exposure to the weather and sank under my footsteps. I wobbled and panicked and wanted to return to the car. I took some deep breaths to regain my composure. Mouse looked back at me.

'Are you sure you can manage?' he said. 'I can go without you.'

'I'd rather die with you than risk being murdered by George.'

Mouse choked with laughter and almost fell off the path.

'It's not far. You can do it.'

As the height off the ground increased, I had to fight for my balance. I didn't look down, but kept going somehow, navigating the tricky switchback without falling off the path, and keeping my eye on the top of the bluff. Before I knew it, we were standing on the seagrass on the flat. I could feel the damp patches under my arms where I had sweated, mostly with fear. Mouse grinned at me.

'You're not exactly Sherpa Tensing, but not bad for an old bird,' he said.

'You're spending too much time with Harry.'

'Probably true.'

'Which way?'

'The footpath behind these bushes leads to the Shanty's back door. No one can see you approach. Well, no one except Ryan. He's got CCTV on the roof. I always suspected they were doing something undercover. Who has cameras on their house?'

We hurried along the path and arrived at the back door of the pub. Before I could knock, the door swung open, and Ryan sat there in his chair, shaking his head.

'You can't be here, Tanya. It's too dangerous. This man has already killed two people.'

'But we had to come. Gladys woke up and identified the painting.'

'The painting? Seriously?'

'It turns out that I bought the one Kovacs is looking for at a car boot sale from the woman who lived in the Fitches' house. And I lent it to you for Joy's birthday present.'

Ryan's eyebrows lifted right into his hair line.

'The icon? That's unbelievable. Life really is odd. You'd better come in. I need your help to retrieve it from the safe, but then you have to leave.'

We followed Ryan into the private part of the pub and to the bottom of the stairs. He pointed upwards.

'I couldn't be bothered going upstairs in the lift,' he said to Mouse. 'Run up to the guest room through that door on the right. The safe is on the back wall. I left it open in case Kovacs wanted more cash or valuables. Nothing in the safe is worth more than Joy. Get the icon and bring it downstairs. Then you must go.'

Mouse ran upstairs. I could sense Ryan's fury at our presence in the pub.

'We wouldn't have come,' I said. 'But we tried to call you twice, and your phone wouldn't pick up the call.'

Ryan spun his chair around to face me.

'When was this?'

'About fifteen minutes ago.'

'Try again.'

'Why?'

'Try again, quickly.'

I fumbled with my mobile and dialled his number, but nothing happened. Ryan took his phone out of the side pocket of his wheelchair. He shook it in frustration, but it did not ring. He put it back with a frown.

'A jammer. I should have known. He's isolated the pub by jamming all calls in and out so he can come and go unannounced. There's no time to get away. When Mouse gives me the icon, you must go down to the cellar and hide. Kovacs should arrive at any moment.'

'But how will you tell the police? Mouse and I could take the back path again and warn them.'

'He's a lot more likely to come that way rather than use the open area of the car park, don't you think?'

Mouse descended the staircase carrying the icon. It depicted two saints with overlarge haloes which really resembled bonnets and had a crude wooden frame.

'It doesn't look like much,' said Mouse, handing it to Ryan. 'I expected it to be more splendid.'

'It's worth Joy's life,' said Ryan. 'Come quickly.'

He led us to the trapdoor into the cellar and pressed a button. The trapdoor opened automatically, and we stood on a metal platform which lowered down into the basement among the barrels. Ryan held his finger to his lips.

'Not a word,' he said. 'No matter what you hear. You must promise me to stay put.'

'We promise,' I said. 'Please be careful.'

The world became black as the trapdoor shut over our heads.

Chapter 31

We stood in the darkness, terrified to move in case we bumped into anything or caused a floorboard to creak. Mouse reached out and took my hand. He squeezed it hard as a sharp bang alerted us to the door of the pub being flung open. I couldn't make out the conversation, but the calm rhythms of Ryan's voice stood out against the semi-hysterical ranting coming from Kovacs. The conversation ended with a thud and footsteps walking towards the trapdoor. Mouse squeezed even harder. I shut my eyes and held my breath. Then the footsteps retreated towards the back door. I slowly emptied my lungs still trying not to make a sound. We waited several minutes after the door shut to be sure the coast was clear.

'There must be a light switch somewhere.' I hissed finally.

'I saw it on the left when we came down on the lift,' said Mouse. 'Give me a minute and I'll find it.'

He released my hand, and I had a rush of terror before the light came on, making my eyes shut at the bright bulb swinging from the ceiling. A control panel for the lift was attached to the wall with a ceramic owl sitting on top of it. Mouse whipped his hand back in fright and then poked it with his finger.

'What on earth is that doing there? I thought it was real.'

He pressed the button to open the trapdoor. We rose up to the pub like actors onto a stage and I spotted Ryan lying on the floor beside his wheelchair. He did not move. I crouched over him and checked his pulse. To my relief it pounded strong in his wrist. Mouse filled a glass with water and came over to help me put Ryan back in his chair. After we got him upright, Ryan opened his eyes and groaned.

'Is he gone? The bastard pistol whipped me. I gave him the icon and begged him to tell me where he had imprisoned Joy. He wouldn't say anything. He lashed out at me and left.'

'We must find him. Try calling George,' I said to Mouse. 'Kovacs won't be able to jam the signal now he's further from the pub.'

Ryan sipped his water, and I dabbed at a cut on his head with a clean tissue while Mouse tried to get through. Finally, George answered.

'Where the hell are you?'

'We're in the pub. Kovacs took the icon and left.'

'What? Stay there. I'll get the station to put out another BOLO on him.'

Minutes later, he burst through the door with a man I didn't recognise who wore a bullet-proof vest, a belt full of stun grenades with a walkie-talkie and carried an enormous gun.

'Is the suspect gone?' he said.

'Out the back,' said Mouse. 'I'll show you.'

'Clear,' he shouted into his walkie-talkie. 'Come round the back.'

They disappeared. George examined Ryan's head.

'That's going to need a stitch. What on earth happened, and why are you here?' he asked me.

'Kovacs used a jamming device,' said Ryan. 'Tanya found out the painting he wanted was the icon she gave me for Joy. When her call wouldn't go through to me, she came to tell me instead. She wanted to save Joy. It's not her fault.'

'Damn it, Tan,' said George. 'He could have hurt you or Mouse while we were right outside. We had a chance to seize him and now he's on the loose again.'

'Will he hurt Joy?' said Ryan. 'He's got what he asked for.'

'I hope not.'

George sank into a chair and took out his phone.

'Any sign of him? Damn it. We were so close. Put up roadblocks. Get Antrim to help with his men.'

He hung up and released a giant sigh. Ryan sat quietly in his chair, his face rigid. I didn't want to disturb him. What could I say? His wife had been kidnapped by a maniac, and we still didn't have any idea where she was being held. I made myself useful and boiled a kettle. While I set out the mugs and milk jug and spoons, I racked my brains for a clue which would turn the situation around, but Kovacs held all the cards. I wondered if we would ever see Joy alive again. Poor Joy. Even her spirit would flag under these circumstances. I had to bite my lip to prevent myself from crying.

The back door opened, and Mouse returned. He glanced around, as if judging the mood.

'Dad. Um, there's something I have to tell you. Please don't be cross.'

George rolled his eyes.

'What now? Did Kovacs steal Ed Murray's fishing boat?'

'No. It's the icon. I, erm, attached a tracker under the frame, and, um, I've got a signal.'

George leapt to his feet.

'Why didn't you say so, you brilliant boy? We're not finished yet. Hand over your phone.'

'I can't. It will switch off if I'm not around and it only opens with my fingerprint.'

George blew out an exasperated breath.

'There's always some reason you need to interfere in my cases. Okay. Let's go in your Mini, Tan, so Kovacs won't know he's been compromised. I'll tell the rest to follow us at a distance using my radio signal. With any luck, he won't even be checking. He thinks he got away with it.'

'Why murder two people for a bog-standard icon?' said Mouse.

'It may be worth a lot of money,' I said. 'I had planned on having it valued after a man got excited when he saw it on the wall of the shop.'

'Could that man have been Kovacs?' said George. 'Maybe that's why he paid Styles to rob the shop and why Styles came out empty-handed.'

He called Joe Brennan on his mobile.

'Joe, my fantastic son has put a tracker on Kovacs. We are going to follow him in the Mini. Can you folks follow us at a discreet distance? Also, can you ring Nick Styles and ask him what he was hired to steal from Second Home? Exactly what did Kovacs ask him for? Thanks.'

He turned to Ryan.

'Will you be okay here? I need someone on site in case Joy turns up. Shall I leave an officer with you?'

'No, it's not necessary. Rescue Joy before it's too late.'

'Where's the car, Tan?'

Mouse laughed.

'I hope you've got your crampons,' he said. 'it's quite steep.'

We walked to the bluff. George turned pale when he took in the steep path, but he didn't falter. He started down it as nimble as a mountain goat with Mouse and me struggling to keep up. At one stage I sat down in the mud and got a big splodge on my jeans. When we reached the bottom, George had a smug look on his face.

'Let's go then,' he said. 'Maybe you should put a bag on your seat to keep the mud off. And put your foot down. He's got a head start on us.'

We piled in with Mouse sitting in the back, monitoring his phone.

'I think he's on foot,' he said. 'He hasn't gone far yet.'

I drove as fast as I dared down the potholed and slippery gravel road. We were closing in on Kovacs at a rate of knots, but then he speeded up.

'It looks like he is driving now,' said Mouse. 'Take a left at the next roundabout.'

I looked in the rearview mirror, but I couldn't see the patrol cars behind us. Joe Brennan and his men were sticking to the plan. I crossed metaphorical fingers for Joy's safety. At least we were close behind. Maybe the police could storm the house before anyone got hurt. Large wet drops fell on the windscreen as storm clouds blew in over the coast. Soon we were driving through a sheet of rain, which reduced visibility near to zero. The afternoon turned dark and forbidding as we drove into the gloom. After a few miles, Kovacs drove down a tiny country lane with overhanging trees which diverted the rain with their leaves. I tried not to get close enough for him to spot us.

'I know where we are,' said Mouse. 'There's an abandoned fisherman's cottage down this road. Do you think that's where he has Joy? I can send Joe the co-ordinates from Google Maps.'

'If you're sure,' said George.

'It's the only house down this lane.'

I didn't like to ask him how he knew about the cottage. I presumed he used it for nefarious purposes with his posse in the years when he strayed slightly off the tracks. Mouse grunted as he spotted Kovac's vehicle arrive at the cottage.

'Stop here, Mum. The cottage is about one hundred metres away.'

'We should wait for my men to get into position,' said George.

'But what about Joy?' I said. 'We can't let Kovacs hurt her. Maybe we can distract him?'

'He's armed. We have to wait. They won't be more than two minutes behind. I expect Joe called in a helicopter too.'

The next few minutes were purgatory as we listened for the sound of the chopper. I wished we had Harry with us. He would be annoyed when he learned we had been in the thick of things without him. A sharp tap on George's window made us all jump. The armed man who had been at the Shanty stood outside my car. George nodded and got out.

'Do not leave the car. We will deal with this. Understood?'

'Understood.'

He disappeared into the rain.

Chapter 32

Rain thundered down on the roof of the Mini, making conversation impossible. Mouse moved into the passenger seat and switched on the windscreen wipers, which were almost useless against the torrent. Minutes passed as we waited impatiently, trapped by our impotence. I watched some damp pigeons huddling together on a branch, their heads nodding as they squabbled over the dryest spots. Then the rain stopped almost as rapidly as it had started and the clouds ahead opened to let rays of sun through them, like a leak in the floor of heaven.

I was so mesmerised by this sight that I didn't notice someone coming out of the cottage towards us. Then George appeared in front of us silhouetted against the sunlight and beckoned us to follow him. Surprised not to see Joy, I felt dread grip my heart as I exited the car and sploshed my way down the lane. I could hear Mouse muttering about his favourite sneakers behind me, but I didn't turn around to sympathise. A strong odour of petrichor hung in the air. The low, whitewashed cottage stood stark against the dark vegetation, its door hanging off its hinges. I couldn't tell the damage had been inflicted.

We followed George inside where several armed coppers loitered on old kitchen chairs, some with missing spindles, which were scattered around a battered oak table. A man I recognised from his photograph sat between them; his hands bound with plastic ties, which appeared uncomfortably tight. The police were taking no chances with their prisoner.

'This is Jonas Kovacs,' said George. 'Gladys's nephew. I want to ask him about Joy before we take him to the station. Can you record our conversation on your phone please, Andrew? Mine is low on battery.'

For once, Mouse didn't complain about George's use of his real name. He took out his phone and put it on the table between them. Then he stood back against the wall, watchful. He had never seen his father interrogate anyone before. George pulled up a chair and folded his arms, staring at Kovacs with contempt in his eyes. He stayed perfectly still until Kovacs broke.

'I won't answer questions,' he said, trying to shuffle his chair away from the table. 'I know my rights.'

'We need you to tell us where Joy is,' said George. 'Her husband is worried about her.'

'The cripple? He's a brave man. I didn't expect to find him alone in the pub with no one to help him.'

'Why did you hit him?' I asked.

'Because I felt like it. You don't understand. How could you?'

'We know your uncle died of starvation to keep your father alive.'

Kovacs's eyes filled with tears, and he tried to extract his hands from the cable ties.

'How do you know that? Who are you?'

'I'm a friend of your Aunt Gladys.'

'Where is she?' he said, twisting in his seat. 'Hasn't she come to laugh at me?'

'Why would she do that?' said George.

'She escaped it all. The starvation, the beatings, the banishment to Germany, the random punishments from the Schmidts, the hatred I suffered for being Jewish. All while she lived her happy English life. I hate her! She took all our family money with her to England. She never came back for my father. She left him to rot.'

He panted with exertion, his face contorted with emotion. I spoke gently to him.

'Gladys didn't know her brothers existed until last week. Your mother sent her to Britain as a baby. Your father and uncle were born after she left. And nobody ever told her about them.'

'And our money?'

'Her adoptive family took it all. They sold the valuable pieces in car boot sales. They had no idea what they were doing. Gladys was a little girl. She's not responsible for this. If your father was badly treated, his adoptive parents are to blame, not Gladys.'

Kovacs shook his head.

'But my father told me she didn't care about us, that she stole our inheritance. I promised him I'd get revenge.'

'Is that why you killed Sandor Sabyani?'

'He laughed at me. I asked him where to find Gladys and he pretended not to know her. I lost my temper.'

'He had dementia,' I said. 'And he divorced Gladys about fifty years ago.'

'Dementia? I—'

'And Sophia Forrest? What had she ever done to you?' said George.

'She planned to warn Joy about me. I only wanted to scare her away, but she fought me, and she fell. Her head hit a rock. I didn't mean to kill her. I thought she was only injured.'

'You left her to die,' said George. 'And my coroner says she had multiple blows to the back of her head. Did she bounce or did you lose your temper again?'

Kovacs flashed him a look of hatred.

'She deserved it. That whole family were thieves—'

'Where's Joy?' said George, interrupting him.

'I don't know.'

'You sent a ransom note to Ryan telling him you were holding her.'

'So? People lie.'

'Is she in danger?'

Kovacs laughed.

'I expect so. If that Soviet agent got hold of her, she's in trouble.'

'Peskov?' I said.

He looked startled.

'You get around, don't you? How do you know about Peskov?'

'He was following us in Budapest.'

'He's insane, you know. He'll kill her.'

'You've got to help us find her.'

'I don't have to do anything. I want a lawyer.'

Kovacs clammed up completely at this point, and George could not get another word out of him. Eventually he gave up and signalled to two burly officers who took Kovacs out to a Black Maria still muttering about Gladys and legacies. They swapped the ties for handcuffs before loading him into the back.

'How will we find Joy without him?' said Mouse.

George shrugged.

'I have no idea. Tanya, can you talk to Ryan for me? Maybe he's heard something from Joy while we've been here. Meanwhile, we need to question Kovacs about the murders in the station with a solicitor present. I'm presuming he'll want us to appoint one, but finding a suitable person is not always possible. Our budget doesn't stretch to it.'

'Do you want a lift to the station?' I said.

'No thanks. I'll hop into a squad car. Will you be okay?'

'Yes, I'll check on Ryan and tell him about Kovacs.'

'I'll need to interview him later. Tell him I'll let him know when he should return to the station.'

We drove back along the wet lanes in almost total silence. Mouse fiddled with his earphones and pretended to listen to music. Finally, he put his phone away.

'What can we do about Joy?'

'First, we must discover where she is. Can you text Ryan and tell him Kovacs didn't have Joy? It will give him time to digest the news before we get there. I don't want it to be a shock.'

'Okay. Anything else?'

'Sure, ask him to find out from his MI6 buddies if Joy flew home to England or not? Tell him we'll be there shortly and ask him if he needs a takeaway.'

I noticed how the prospect of helping made him relax immediately. He had a lot in common with Harry, despite them not being related, but he got his 'isms' from George. I followed my nose back to Seacastle, and we stopped at Greggs to load up on sausage rolls, chicken slices and Danish pastries. I did a circuit of the block while Mouse dashed indoors to buy them.

We also passed by the Grotty Hovel to collect an agitated Harry who had been left out of the loop almost completely and made his displeasure known. He calmed down after wolfing a sausage roll, which told me he had been concerned and hungry rather than actually cross with us. I promised to tell him all about our morning but asked him to wait until we reached the Shanty, so I didn't have to do it twice.

'Which way are we going to the Shanty?' asked Mouse, making me snort with laughter.

'I feel as if I missed all the fun,' said Harry.

I didn't reply. We pulled into the car park and took the large bag of goodies along the dodgy path to the Shanty. We found Ryan waiting for us outside the door, taking in the last few rays of the afternoon sun. He greeted us and we followed him inside, where he had set out a table with a large pot of tea.

'I thought we'd eat first and then have a drink as the sun goes down over Pirate's Harbour,' he said.

'I'm so sorry about Joy,' I said. 'At least Kovacs didn't get his hands on her.'

'She's a lot safer now he's out of the picture,' said Ryan. 'Don't worry, we'll find her. My mates at HQ are checking the flight manifestos and safe houses right now.'

'Can I help?' said Mouse.

'Leave it to them. They've got the best kit on the planet.'

'Please tell us what happened with Kovacs,' said Harry. 'I can't believe you faced him without me.'

'We were in the car the whole time,' said Mouse. 'We just gave George a lift.'

'I still want to hear about it.'

'Me too,' said Ryan. 'Let's make short work of these delicious goodies. I can smell them from here.'

The men scoffed down the pastries and drank tea while I related the happenings of the day. Mouse saved me a sausage roll before they all disappeared. Ryan shook his head in disbelief.

'It's hard to belief this was caused by Joy trying to connect with her family. Those TV programmes never have kidnappings and murders in them.'

'Maybe they keep those quiet,' said Harry.

'I can't imagine where Joy is,' said Ryan. 'It's not out of character for her to be incommunicado, but she usually tells me first. I guess we'll find out soon.'

Chapter 33

Mouse and I visited Gladys the next day in the hospital, but did not give her many details on the drama. We told her Joy had been delayed in Hungary. Gladys did not take Joy's disappearance well and tried to get out of her hospital bed despite being under strict instructions to stay there.

'I've got to find Joy,' she said. 'She would have said something if her plans had changed.'

'Not to you. She doesn't know who you are yet,' said Mouse, earning a scowl.

'Ryan says she often goes off grid. There's nothing to be concerned about,' I said, lying, when I had done nothing but worry for days.

'And they won't let you go home yet,' said Mouse. 'What's wrong with you anyway?'

'I've got some sort of heart thing,' said Gladys, gesticulating at the tubes and wires connected to her. 'They won't let me out until they're sure I won't drop dead on the pavement.'

'You already tried that,' said Mouse, laughing.

Gladys grimaced.

'Cheeky boy. Haven't you taught him any manners?'

'I'm afraid I got him too late. You can blame George,' I said.

'Hasn't George managed to get any information out of that Kovacs fellow yet? Couldn't he waterboard him or something?'

'Not that you know what that means,' I said.

'I've got Google on my phone,' said Gladys.

'And she's not afraid to use it,' said Mouse, ducking as she tried to hit him.

'We've got to go now,' I said. 'Please behave. We want you to get better soon.'

Gladys grabbed my hand.

'Please find my girl. I couldn't bear to lose her now. I just couldn't.'

I nodded, unable to tell her how little I could do to find Joy. If Ryan and his network hadn't located her, I didn't know what to do.

We left Gladys to sulk in bed and went to Second Home where Roz and Ghita were waiting for us. I had not told them much about the whole Kovacs fake kidnapping drama, but the fact Joy had not returned had made them suspicious they were being left out of the loop. I bought fresh chocolate croissants, which filled the car with a heavenly aroma, as a peace offering. The two women leapt upon us with cries of glee and took the paper bag when they spotted the logo.

'Guess who popped in for a browse yesterday,' said Roz, taking a large bite and getting chocolate on her chin. 'Miles Quirk.'

'Miles who? Oh, Grace's friend. What did he want?'

'He bought the Limoge Art Deco tea set you got from Elsie Riley's house clearance. I charged him a fortune,' said Ghita, smirking.

'He didn't mind,' said Roz. 'He can charge his client double.'

'Anyway, we don't care about the shop, we want to know about Joy,' said Ghita. 'I thought she was supposed to come home straight after you.'

'So did I,' said Mouse.

'Oo, is it something to do with their job?' said Roz. 'The whole town is on tenterhooks.'

'And who told the town about their secret?' I said, raising an eyebrow.

Roz blushed.

'You didn't seriously expect me to keep that to myself, did you?'

'I did actually, but I guess this was their last mission, one way or another.'

'Is there no one who can help?' said Ghita. 'Didn't you make friends with that man who owns the bookshop in Budapest?'

'Imre? Yes, but he only knows what we do.'

'I still think you should call him,' said Roz. 'I bet he doesn't know Joy didn't turn up in England.'

'I'll ask Ryan what he thinks,' I said. 'After all, the ball's back in his court now Kovacs has been arrested.'

'It doesn't add up somehow. It looks as if Joy's last mission has turned political after all.'

Ryan turned up at the shop after I called him, as he had come into town to buy an electric pulley.

'For the lift,' he said.

'I thought you had all the parts in your cellar,' I said.

'Nearly all. You know how I love a project.'

'Any news from Joy?'

His face fell.

'Not yet. Joy never left Hungary. Since she missed her flight out, there's no sign of her on any other flight manifesto.'

'But what's she still doing in Budapest?' I said.

'Someone or something may be preventing her from leaving,' said Ryan. 'My contacts are flummoxed. They think she may have been using a safe house, but she's disappeared.'

'Have you spoken to Imre?'

'No, I've been trying to do this through official channels and he's not an official contact. I think it may be time to call him anyway. Will you do it?'

'Okay, give me a second.'

I took out my phone and dialled his number.

'Tanya? I was just about to call you. Magda, the receptionist from your hotel, contacted me just now. She told me Joy showed up last night. Joy got into a taxi to go to the airport this morning and told Magda she would confirm her arrival in England. Magda told me she didn't hear from Joy and checked the CCTV of the street outside. She noticed the taxi driver wearing a flat cap. She's in a complete panic as she's convinced it was Peskov.'

'How come Joy didn't recognise him?'

'I don't know, but I received an anonymous text after Magda's call telling me Joy had been kidnapped. The text demanded fifty thousand euros ransom.'

'Let us know if you receive any more messages. We'll make a plan and get back to you shortly,' I said, hanging up.

'What did he say?' said Ryan, pale as a ghost.

'Imre, the owner of the bookshop. He thinks Peskov's got Joy. He's asked for a ransom.'

Harry arrived as I was speaking. He shook his head.

'I told you he was dodgy. I should've dealt with him properly when I had the chance.'

'We left Budapest too soon.'

Chapter 34

Ryan had no problems getting the ransom money together. I didn't ask him where he laid his hands on so much cash, but I presumed MI6 had stumped up. We booked tickets back to Budapest the next day. Harry did not attempt to convince me to stay at home.

'Why would I waste my time?' he said, but he hugged me close.

Mouse did not appreciate being left in Seacastle to guard Gladys and Hades, but George forbade me to take him with us. I was glad of the excuse. I suspected the trip would be dangerous, and I didn't want to risk anything happening to him. Ryan came with us despite the difficulties with logistics. He had to be taken up to the aircraft on the goods lift in his chair and then Harry lifted him into his seat in the front row while his chair got stowed in the hold. It had never occurred to me how difficult Ryan had found it to travel since his accident. His career had petered out as a result and Joy had been travelling far more than him. From what George had relayed, she had always been top dog in the spying game. Now she had been targeted by a rival who was jealous of her success.

We travelled into town in an Uber van with a wheelchair space in it. I had already ensured Ryan had a room on the ground floor at the Grand Hotel, so there would be no awkward moments caused by the lack of a lift. I texted Imre from the van telling him we had arrived in Budapest, but he didn't reply. Magda welcomed us with hugs and became quite emotional when she met Ryan. She shed tears while relating how she had recognised the driver of the taxi too late to save Joy from his clutches.

'Imre's waiting for you at his bookshop,' she said. 'Oh dear, I hope he's heard from Peskov. I feel responsible.'

'Please don't say that. You may have saved her life by recognising him. We're only here because of you,' said Ryan.

She gave a weak smile. We dispersed up to our rooms to leave our bags. I noticed we were all on the lower floors this time. Perhaps only new guests had to climb up to the top floors. Then a thought occurred to me.

'Why didn't this occur to me earlier?' I said to Harry.

'What?'

But I had already gone, running back down the stairs to reception where Magda moped over a magazine. She gasped in surprise when I skidded to a halt on the tiled floor.

'Does Joy have a permanent room here where she keeps her things?'

'She does, but I can't let you in. I'd get fired.'

'What about me?' said Ryan, gliding up. 'Surely I can enter? I'm her husband after all.'

Magda wrung her hands.

'Oh, well, I suppose so. Be careful you don't break anything in there.'

'What on earth would we break?' said Harry.

I shrugged and took the key from Magda. We followed a back corridor. Joy's room was beside the emergency exit. Not a coincidence, I thought. I opened the room, but I let Ryan enter first, in case there was anything we shouldn't see. A yelp of surprise was followed by a roar of laughter before he beckoned us in. I wasn't sure what to expect, but a numerous flock of porcelain and ceramic owls did not figure high on my list of guesses.

'What on earth?' said Harry. 'I didn't know Joy had an owl fetish.'

Ryan spun around in his chair, grinning as he took it all in.

'A parliament of owls. I should have known. She never let me stay in her room, you know?'

'But why didn't she tell you?' I asked.

'It's my fault. She brought one home a few years ago, and I made her put it in the cellar. I never thought…'

'We'll get her back, mate,' said Harry. 'Come on. Let's see Imre.'

We left Joy's room as we found it, after discovering no clues as to her whereabouts. I noticed Ryan putting something in the pocket of his wheelchair, but he didn't mention it to us, so I didn't comment. We made the short walk to Imre's shop without incident, but found it closed.

'Where is he?' said Harry. 'I thought Magda said he'd be waiting for us.'

'She did. Can you see anything through the window?'

Harry leaned against the glass as he tried to peer into the shop.

'I can't see anything,' he said. 'Has Peskov taken him too?'

'Wait,' I said. 'Be careful. Don't rub the glass. There's something written there. Breathe on it again.'

Sure enough, a word appeared in the condensation and disappeared almost immediately.

'Do it again,' said Ryan.

'Pala something,' I said. 'It says Palatin, I think.'

'I don't think Joy knows anyone of that name,' said Ryan. 'How can we be sure Imre wrote it?'

'We can't,' said Harry. 'But it's our only clue.'

'It's rather cryptic,' said Ryan. 'I do the Telegraph crossword, and I have no idea what it means.'

'Cryptic? Wait, I know where they are,' I said. 'The Palatine Crypt. I read about it in my Budapest guidebook.'

'Where's that?' said Harry

'It's under Buda Castle. Some members of the Habsburg family are buried there. It's closed for restoration, but we can get in through the caves. Imre showed me once,' said Ryan.

'I'll call an Uber.'

As luck would have it, we got another Uber van with a space for Ryan's wheelchair inside. The driver took us over the Chain bridge and dropped us beside the steep sided limestone platform on which the castle stood.

'Follow me,' said Ryan, entering a fault line in the limestone, which didn't seem to lead anywhere.

As we got to the end, I noticed a small entrance overhung with rock. Its position meant it could not be seen from the road.

'Open Sesame,' said Ryan. 'It's a bit of a squeeze, but I think I can get through in the chair.'

As we entered the narrow passageway, the temperature dropped like a stone. I shivered, whether with cold or fear, I couldn't be sure. I used the torch on my phone to illuminate our path. Our footsteps echoed in the darkness. Ryan grunted with effort as he manoeuvred his wheelchair through the gaps in the rock. Harry walked behind him, trying to help get him through.

'I guess they didn't have disabled access in the dark ages,' Ryan muttered.

'Maybe they didn't have full-service chariots,' said Harry. 'You could outfit a house with the stuff you carry around.'

Ryan laughed.

'True.'

A metallic sound rang up ahead of us and I held up my hand to shut them up.

'I heard something. We must be close.'

The mechanical whirr from Ryan's chair became more obvious in the complete silence which surrounded us. We could not return now. I steeled myself and pointed the torch to the floor, so it didn't shine into the crypt when we arrived. Suddenly the passageway opened out into a chamber with a black and white tiled floor and rounded, vaulted Art Nouveau, blue painted ceilings sprinkled with gold stars, and with painted plant borders and angel motifs in the corners. At one end, a massive bronze angel with outstretched wings held a lonely vigil over the white marble sarcophagi containing Archduke Joseph Karl and his family, while an enormous statue of him sat at the centre of the crypt. I stared in wonder at the beautiful decoration, quite forgetting why I was there.

A familiar voice with a thick Russian accent broke through my contemplation.

'Ah, Mr Wells, I presume, good of you to join us. Your wife is most anxious to see you again before she dies.'

A whimper came from behind one tomb and I saw Joy trussed up with rope, leaning against a tiny sarcophagus. She had a gag in her mouth and a tear ran down her cheek as she struggled to speak. I gave her an encouraging smile, but my heart sunk as Peskov emerged from behind a larger tomb carrying a pistol of some sort.

'Did you bring the money?' he said.

'What money?' said Ryan. 'Nobody mentioned money to me.'

'You think this is a treasure hunt? You're supposed to bring the ransom.'

His voice rose high and indignant. He wobbled and grabbed the edge of the tomb. I wondered if he was drunk.

'Where's Imre?' I said.

'Oh, he's here somewhere. Stupid librarian thought he was a hero. Nobody gets to be a hero except me.'

He stared at Harry and raised his gun. 'And you, Mr Tough Guy. You don't look so tough now, do you?'

Harry did not move, but I could almost sense his blood boiling. Instead, Ryan guided his wheelchair forward, putting it between us and Peskov.

'You need to let these people go. They are not involved.'

'They are now. I can't let anyone leave here alive if you don't have my money.'

Ryan shrugged.

'I lied,' he said. 'if you search in the back pocket of my wheelchair, you'll find the money in there.'

'Take it out,' said Peskov, waving his pistol.

'I can't reach it. You'll have to get it yourself.'

'You. Woman. You get it for me, and don't try any funny stuff.'

I froze. 'Me, but—'

'Get the money or your friend dies.'

He pointed the pistol at Harry again.

I forced my legs to move and took some stiff-legged steps towards Ryan. I bent down to reach into the back pocket of his wheelchair. He whispered in my ear, 'Pick up the Taser and hold it under the money packet. When Peskov takes the money, press the button and shock him. Don't worry about the gun. He'll spasm and drop it.'

'Seriously, who do you think I am? Mata Hari?'

'Harry tells me you're her twin sister. You can do it.'

'Stop whispering. You think I can't hear you? Bullets are stronger than words.'

I gave Harry a loving glance and walked towards Peskov. Harry tried to run at Peskov, but Ryan swung the chair into his path. Harry swore under his breath as he flew through the air and rolled to break his fall. This distracted Peskov long enough for me to shoot the Taser at his ribs. His eyes came out on stalks as he froze and collapsed on the floor, the gun flying away from him towards Harry. He picked it up and put on the safety catch, arching an eyebrow at me and shaking his head. I dropped the money packet on the ground and untied Joy. First, I removed the gag, so she could breathe more freely, and then I undid the rope binding her ankles and wrists. He had hogtied her, and she took a while to stand as her blood ran to her extremities again. Ryan wheeled up to her and held out his arms. She sat on his lap and kissed him again and again.

'I'm so glad you're here,' she said. 'I've never been rescued by the Cavalry before.'

'Where's Imre?' I asked.

'Over there. He hasn't moved. I hope…'

Harry went to Imre's side. He took his pulse and put him in the recovery position.

'I think he's okay. He's got a nasty bump on his head though, so we'd better take him to hospital.'

'How did you get in here?' I asked Joy.

'We came through the door. It's not locked.'

'What about Peskov?' said Harry.

'Honestly? Just leave him here with the money. I don't want it. I need him to leave us alone.'

Imre stirred and stared up at the ceiling.

'Am I in heaven?' he said.

'Funny angels,' said Ryan, laughing.

'We left our wings at home,' said Harry.

'Can you stand?' I asked.

'I think so. If Harry can give me a hand. Then I'll take a taxi to the hospital. I think Joy needs something to eat. Peskov starved her.'

We staggered out of the castle under the curious gaze of a Japanese tour group who seemed to think we were the crew of a reality show. Some of them broke into a tentative applause. Harry even signed an autograph. Joy walked alongside Ryan's wheelchair and would not let go of his hand. The sun was going down as we crossed the Danube, so we headed for 0.75 on St Stephen's Basilica square. We got a table outside and enjoy the balmy evening. Joy seemed to re-inflate with food. She blushed when Ryan asked her about the owls.

'Please bring them home with us,' said Ryan. 'I promise to rescue the one in the cellar.'

'I saw that one,' I said. 'It gave me quite a turn.'

'What were you doing in the cellar?' said Joy.

'It's a long story. But it's not mine to tell. Can you bear to wait until we get back to England?'

Chapter 35

We spend a pleasant couple of days in Budapest before leaving again. Harry and I paid another visit to the Gellert Baths, and we all ate far too much at the breakfast café. Imre had recovered from his concussion and spent time with Harry reviewing his collection of Cold War literature. Ryan spent most of his time with Joy who recuperated in her room and packed her owls to take home. Their happiness at being together again shone out of every pore, but Joy couldn't help mourning her lack of progress in finding Miriam Steinberg, unaware she already knew her. I found keeping quiet about Gladys almost impossible, but I respected her wish to tell Joy herself. Mouse gave me progress reports on Gladys who, to her chagrin, could not yet leave the hospital after her collapse. The nurses were taking no chances with her health after Mouse let slip about her lost daughter coming home.

Joy bought a seat on the same flight as us and we all flew back to England two days after her rescue. Imre controlled his crush and wished us all goodbye without crying. I felt sorry for him. Unrequited love is the worst sort. The anticipation of Joy's reunion with Gladys made me agitated on the way home. Harry knew exactly what was wrong with me, but he pretended to be perplexed.

'Have you got ants in your pants?' he asked.

'Don't be silly.'

'I thought you liked me to be silly.'

'Not right now. I may burst at high altitude.'

The two-hour flight took for ever. We had to go through the entire performance with Ryan's chair twice, which didn't help. The air crew were great and made him feel completely at ease despite the personal nature of the manoeuvre. Harry transferred him to his chair each time, and I notice how carefully he lifted Ryan and placed him in his seat.

'You're just a great big softy, Harry Fletcher,' said Joy.

'Don't tell anyone,' said Harry. 'I've got my reputation to think of.'

We parted at the Seacastle railway station. Joy and Ryan headed for the Shanty and Harry and I for the Grotty Hovel. I texted Mouse and warned him we were on our way, and he opened the door of the Grotty Hovel before I could put my key in the door.

'It's fantastic you found her,' he said. 'Does she know about Gladys yet?'

'No, but we're trying to get Joy to visit Gladys in hospital. I think I'll ask her to go with me on some pretext,'

'Why don't you tell her Gladys knew her mother and has some information for her?'

'Are you joking?'

'No, I'm serious. It will put Joy in the right frame of mind to receive the news.'

I mulled over the idea and decided Mouse was right. Joy did not suspect a thing, and in fact seemed elated when I picked her up the following day in the Mini.

'What an amazing coincidence Gladys knew my mother! I suppose she'd be about the same age. It's unbelievable.'

'Sure is,' I said, swallowing a smirk.

'What if she has a photograph of them together? I'm so excited. I can't believe I searched for Miriam in Budapest, but she was here all the time.'

She became quiet for a while.

'Are you okay?' I asked.

'What if she's dead?'

'Oh, I hope not,' I said.

It's never been so hard to maintain a poker face. Luckily, Joy was so involved in her own thoughts, she didn't notice me fighting with my emotions. We left the Mini in the car park and walked through reception. Joy reminded me of Ghita, the way she bounced on her tiptoes in the lift. She almost destroyed the flowers she had brought with her by shaking the bunch with excitement.

'I hope Gladys likes shabby chic,' she said, examining them with a rueful expression.

We walked into Gladys's ward, and I noticed Gladys had moved from her bed to an armchair near the window. She stared out of the window at the branches waving in the breeze and did not hear us approach. I touched her freckled arm, and she turned around. Her eyes filled with instant tears as she gazed mesmerised at her daughter. I was struck by the resemblance between them. Why didn't I notice it before? The slight tilt of the nose, the sharp blue eyes, the small pink lips.

'Hello,' said Joy. 'I brought you these. They got damaged in my excitement to hear about my mother. I'm sorry.'

'They are the most beautiful flowers I have ever received.'

Joy's face registered her confusion.

'I don't understand. Are you being sarcastic?'

'How could I be? Please sit down.'

'I'll sit over there,' I said, gesticulating at a chair between the next two beds.

'There's no need for that,' said Joy. 'I may need moral support. Please stay.'

I looked at Gladys for help, but she had focussed on Joy and had forgotten about me. I perched on the edge of Gladys's bed.

'I hear you travelled to Budapest to look for your mother,' said Gladys.

'Yes, that's right. But I hit a dead end. I wasn't aware of the drama at home. Ryan didn't tell me about Sophia being my sister. He only said I was in danger and told me to stay in Budapest until he worked out the reasons behind the murder. And then, of course, Peskov showed up and things became a lot more complicated. I had no idea my mother had been taken to England and adopted. I don't have a present name for her, so I'm a bit stuck. Tanya told me you knew her. Is that true?'

'Oh yes. I knew Miriam very well—'

'Is she still alive?'

Gladys laughed.

'Barely. But she's recovering.'

Joy looked annoyed.

'Why are you talking in riddles? I've waited years for this day. What is my mother's name?'

Gladys bit her lip and took a deep breath.

'Gladys Fitch. Her name is Gladys Fitch.'

Joy gasped and her hand flew to her mouth.

'What? You? Please don't joke with me. I couldn't bear it.'

Gladys looked as if she would break into pieces. She reached out a wrinkled hand and patted Joy's knee.

'It's me, Joy. I'm your mummy. Honestly.' She swallowed down a sob. 'Please don't hate me. They made me give you away. In those days, you had no choice.'

Joy shoved her chair back and stood up ramrod straight. She gulped several times, and I handed her a tissue.

'You knew?' she said to me.

I nodded, almost flinching from her accusing glance.

'I'm afraid so. I wanted to tell you, but Gladys needed to do that herself.'

'How did you find me?' said Joy.

'Mouse,' said Gladys.

'That boy,' said Joy. 'He has saved our lives.'

Gladys held out her arms and Joy sank to her knees to be received in her embrace. Joy lowered her head on to Gladys's chest and sobbed while Gladys stroked her head and murmured loving words in her ear. I found they weren't the only people crying. I wept my heart out, remembering my mother and how lucky I was to have her, despite her obsession with the Squander Bug and eating mouldy food. I found the strength to stand up.

'I'm going now,' I said, but no one was listening.

I got in the car and drove to Second Home where Mouse was loitering with Ghita and Roz, still trying to get their speaker to link to their phones. The gales of laughter hit me as I opened the door, and I let them wash over me, luxuriating in the healing waves of giggles. Mouse came bouncing down the stairs. He took one look at me and assessed my puffy face.

'Were they happy to be reunited?' he asked.

'Ecstatic,' I said, my nose running again.

'Why are your eyes leaking?' he said. 'Come here, Mum. You need a hug.'

'They blamed you,' I said, burying my face in his shoulder.

Chapter 36

Over the next few days, our world experienced several contortions before righting itself again. Ryan waited patiently while Joy and Gladys shut themselves away to reconnect and find a way of going forward together. Joy had not been told the entire story about Janos Steinberg yet. She found it hard enough to take in the news about Sandor and Sophia. Losing a half-sister you never knew, who died coming to warn you about being in danger, brought up many emotions the normally positive Joy found difficult to deal with. We all rallied round to make it easier on her.

Meanwhile, Ryan found a valuer who could assess the worth of the icon. I certainly didn't want it back. It seemed obvious to me who it belonged to.

'Joy should keep it, since it's her legacy from Erzsébet anyway,' I said.

'That's not the point,' he said. 'After all, you bought it. Without you it would have gone missing for ever.'

We waited with bated breath while the little man ummed and ahed over the icon, examining it with a large Sherlock Holmes type magnifying glass. Finally, he adjusted his pince-nez and looked over the top over the top of it.

'It's worth about a hundred quid,' said the valuer. 'I'm charging you half that for coming.'

I don't know which of us was more shocked by the discovery the icon was a cheap copy with little intrinsic value. I couldn't get over the fact Janos had killed two people for it. How did the Cook sisters persuade the authorities to let Gladys stay in Britain without the money to satisfy the conditions of her visa? Maybe it would always be a mystery. Ryan just laughed when he found out and gave me the money.

'Why don't we try having that birthday party again tomorrow?' he said.

Gathering a bunch of friends together for a night at the pub is the easiest thing in the world, especially when it's a mixture of celebration and drama. Roz and Ghita were agog at our exploits in Budapest, and ecstatic about Joy and Gladys being mother and daughter. While I had been away, they had sold some of the new stock and entertained a visit from Grace Wong who took away the flapper dresses after paying in cash. Ghita's rhubarb and orange cake had been flying off the shelves, which made her happy.

I called Helen to invite her to the pub. She sounded grumpy with me, but I knew she was just cross at me for going back to Budapest to rescue Joy.

'Harry's in the SAS, not you. I don't know why you had to put yourself in danger.'

I lied and told her I had not been in any danger which mollified her.

'You won't believe how worried George was. You two are so funny. You couldn't stand each other when you were married and now you are best buddies.'

'You're not jealous are you?'

'Of course not. He loves me. He only tolerates you.'

I laughed.

'Are you coming to Joy's birthday party?'

'Only if you promise me no more bodies.'

'I think I can promise that.'

Joy's birthday party took place after a lazy day at the shop, consisting of almost unbroken time for coffee and cake and few customers to serve. Roz announced she had to return home for Joy's present, which she had forgotten and to wake Ed who had been on night shift on his fishing boat. I travelled to the party in a taxi with Harry, Mouse and Gladys who glowed with happiness. I couldn't imagine how she felt to be reunited with Joy, but her sparkling eyes spoke volumes about her mood. We pulled up to the car park and headed down the path to the Shanty. The full moon lit our way and turned us all pale with its light. Harry stroked my hair and kissed me when I stopped to gaze at it.

'I'm so in love with you,' he said. 'You're so beautiful and brave.'

I blinked away a tear.

'Don't make me blub,' I said. 'My mascara will run everywhere.'

A roar of noise greeted us as we entered the pub. Joy and Ryan were behind the bar side by side, greeting their guests. They had organised a lock in for Joy's birthday, so only friends had come. I didn't recognise everyone. From the suits, I suspected some of their colleagues had come down from London. Even Terry Antrim had turned up. He gave me a tentative wave, and I beamed back at him without Harry seeing me. Gladys headed straight for the bar, which she slipped behind to give Joy a birthday hug and a bouquet of pink roses. I saw Roz and Ghita signalling us from our favourite table under the window and went to greet them. They were sitting with Helen and George and Flo the pathologist.

Soon we joined the general hubbub, and the night only got better. Ghita disappeared with Mouse to bring an enormous, tiered birthday cake out to a table in the centre of the pub. Everyone sang Happy Birthday to You at full volume, making the walls vibrate with the sound. Joy blushed and cut the cake and then came to sit with us while Mouse and Harry cut the cake for distribution. Ryan let off party poppers and other indoor fireworks and looked happier than I had ever seen him.

'Thank you for saving me,' said Joy. 'I thought I was a goner.'

'Don't be silly. You'd have done the same for us,' I said. 'We had no intention of leaving you there with that ghastly man.'

'You mean Imre,' she said, snorting.

'He has a rather noticeable crush.'

'Don't tell Ryan. He'll invent some sort of secret weapon to blow Imre off the surface of the earth.'

'Whatever happened to Peskov?' I asked.

'Oh, my sources tell me the authorities in Budapest handed him over to the Russian Embassy. I'm sure they dealt with him.'

'I'm sure they did.'

Roz leaned across the table and handed Joy a small present wrapped in pink crepe paper and tied with a purple ribbon.

'Thanks Roz. You shouldn't have bought me anything.'

'Oh, I didn't buy it,' she said. 'Tanya gave it to me. She found it in the same box as the icon. It belonged to your grandmother. I thought you should have it.'

'What about me?' said Gladys.

'You can share it,' said Roz.

'Do you want to open it?' said Joy.

'No, darling. It'll be yours eventually no matter what happens.'

Joy carefully peeled away the layers and found a black Bakelite box inside with white costume gems stuck on the top. She turned it around twice, a perplexed look on her face.

'Don't you like it?' said Roz.

'You can't give me this,' said Joy.

'Why ever not,' said Gladys.

'These are real,' said Joy.

'Diamonds?' I said. 'So that's where they went to.'

'My mother was a genius,' said Gladys.

'So Janos was right,' said Ryan, admiring the box.

'I'd have shared them with him,' said Gladys. 'He didn't have to kill Sandor and Sophia.'

'Well, they're yours now and I vote we give a finder's fee to Second Home for keeping them safe.'

'I'll drink to that,' I said.

'Line them up, Ryan. We've got even more to celebrate,' said Harry, turning to face the crowd and raising his voice. 'I propose a toast to Jozsef and Erzsébet Steinberg. Gone, but never forgotten.'

The entire pub raised their glasses.

'The Steinbergs.'

Everyone cheered. Gladys had tears in her eyes as she hugged Joy. Harry winked at me, and I knew everything would be all right.

Thank you for reading Lethal Secret. Please leave me a review if you enjoyed it.

Loved *Lethal Secret*? Don't miss Tanya's next case! Pre-order Malign Fortune on Amazon and join Tanya as she unravels the truth behind a deadly prediction.

Other books

The Seacastle Mysteries - a cosy mystery series set on the south coast of England

Deadly Return (Book 1)
Staying away is hard, but returning may prove fatal. Tanya Bowe, a former investigative journalist, is adjusting to life as an impoverished divorcee in the seaside town of Seacastle. She crosses paths with a long-lost schoolmate, Melanie Conrad, during a house clearance to find stock for her vintage shop. The two women renew their friendship, but their reunion takes a tragic turn when Mel is found lifeless at the foot of the stairs in the same house.

While the police are quick to label Mel's death as an accident, Tanya's gut tells her there's more to the story. Driven by her instincts, she embarks on her own investigation, delving into Mel's mysterious past. As she probes deep into the Conrad family's secrets, Tanya uncovers a complex web of lies and blackmail. But the further she digs, the more intricate the puzzle becomes. As Tanya's determination grows, so does the shadow of danger. Each new revelation brings her closer to a chilling truth. Can she unravel the secrets surrounding Mel's demise before the killer strikes again?

Eternal Forest (Book 2)
What if proving a friend's husband innocent of murder implicates her instead?

Tanya Bowe, an ex-investigative journalist, and divorcee, runs a vintage shop in the coastal town of Seacastle. When her old friend, Lexi Burlington-Smythe borrows the office above the shop as a base for the campaign to create a kelp sanctuary off the coast, Tanya is thrilled with the chance to get involved and make some extra money. Tanya soon gets drawn into the high-stake arguments surrounding the campaign, as tempers are frayed, and her friends, Roz and Ghita favour opposing camps. When a celebrity eco warrior is murdered, the evidence implicates Roz's husband Ed, and Tanya finds her loyalties stretched to breaking point as she struggles to discover the true identity of the murderer.

Fatal Tribute (Book 3)
How do you find the murderer when every act is convincing?

Tanya Bowe, an ex-investigative journalist, agrees to interview the contestants of the National Talent Competition for the local newspaper, but finds herself up to her neck in secrets, sabotage and simmering resentment. The tensions increase when her condescending sister comes to stay next door for the duration of the contest.

Several rising stars on the circuit hope to win the competition, but old stager, Lance Emerald, is not going down without a fight. When Lance is found dead in his dressing room, Tanya is determined to find the murderer, but complex dynamics between the contestants and fraught family relationships make the mystery harder to solve. **Can Tanya uncover the truth before another murder takes centre stage?**

Toxic Vows (Book 4)
A shotgun marriage can lead to deadly celebrations
Despite her reservations, Tanya Bowe, ex-investigative journalist and local sleuth, feels obliged to plan and attend the wedding of her ex-husband DI George Carter. The atmosphere is less than convivial as underlying tensions bubble to the surface. But when the bride is found dead only hours after the ceremony, the spotlight is firmly turned onto George as the prime suspect. A reluctant Tanya is forced to come to George's aid when his rival, DI Antrim is determined to prove him responsible for her death. She discovers the bride had a lot of dangerous secrets, but so did other guests at the wedding. Did the murderer intend to kill, or have an elaborate plan gone badly wrong?

Mortal Vintage (Book 5)
Does an ancient coven hold the key to solving a murder?
Few tears are shed when the unpopular manager of the annual Seacastle Vintage Fair meets a sinister end. But local sleuth Tanya Bowe is thrust into the heart of the investigation when her friend, Grace Wong, finds herself under scrutiny for the murder. When Tanya's investigation uncovers a suspicious death in the same family, all bets are off. She navigates dark undercurrents of greed and betrayal as she uncovers a labyrinth of potential suspects associated with an ancient coven. Nothing is as it seems, and every clue adds extra complications. To solve the case, Tanya must answer one key question. Did someone hate the

victim enough to kill her, or was greed the stronger motive?

Last Orders (Book 6)
Has a restaurant critic's scathing review led to his murder?
The grand opening of the Surfusion restaurant attracts a famous food critic, raising the stakes for the owners. The night takes a dark turn when he collapses into his coffee, hours after his scathing review goes live. Local sleuth, Tanya Bowe, a friend of the owners, witnesses the shocking incident and vows to clear their names.

As Tanya digs deeper, what at first seems like an open-and-shut case against the owners unravels into a web of intrigue. Is the famous critic even the intended victim of the crime? Tanya Bowe has her work cut out for her as hidden motives lead to simmering tensions among her friends. With time running out and Surfusion's future on the line, can Tanya unmask the culprit before it's too late?

Grave Reality (Book 7)
A reality show turns deadly when death rewrites the script.
Chaos breaks out in the quiet town of Seacastle when the cast and crew of the hit show Sloane Rangers descend upon it, stirring up drama both on and off the screen. Local sleuth and former investigative reporter, Tanya Bowe, is brought on board as a consultant, tasked with recommending perfect filming locations for the episode. Tanya soon uncovers a tangled web of strained relationships and simmering tensions among the cast members. When one of the stars of the show is discovered unconscious in her room, Tanya finds herself at the heart of a complex murder investigation

where everyone is a suspect. Unravelling the truth seems impossible when many of them have difficulty distinguishing real life from the scripted show. As the case unfolds, several beloved cast members emerge as the prime suspects, sending shockwaves through Seacastle. With everyone playing a part and secrets buried deep, the murderer remains hidden in plain sight. Can Tanya unravel the truth before someone else dies?

Malign Fortune (Book 9)
Seacastle's famous medium is dead. Did his secrets kill him?

When a revered spiritualist correctly predicts his own death, his clients are torn between awe and alarm. But the police are calling it murder and one of their own was the last person known to visit him. The case seems open and shut, but local sleuth Tanya Bowe isn't convinced. The medium had a gift for unearthing secrets and a talent for using them to his advantage. As Tanya digs into his murky past, she uncovers a web of manipulation that stretches across Seacastle, leaving behind damaged reputations and bitter grudges. With ex-husband DI George Carter bound to follow the evidence, and his colleague's career hanging by a thread, it's up to Tanya to uncover the truth before another life is destroyed.

Purrfect Crime – A Seacastle Christmas Novella
The purrfect Christmas mystery to keep you up all night.

When preparations for Christmas at the Grotty Hovel are interrupted by the discovery of a body in the back garden, local sleuth, Tanya Bowe, finds herself embroiled in a cold case mystery. The local police are less than enthusiastic about pursuing the case before the holidays, but Tanya can't wait. Then Hades, their rescue cat, goes missing, and all festivities are put on hold as Tanya and her housemates search high and low for their pesky feline. As the hunt for Hades becomes more frantic, Tanya suspects his disappearance may be linked to the body in her garden. Who has kit-napped Hades? Will Tanya find the murderer before the turkey starts to rot?

Other books by the Author
I write under various pen names in different genres. If you are looking for another mystery, why don't you try Mortal Mission, written as Pip Skinner.

Mortal Mission
Will they find life on Mars, or death?
When the science officer for the first crewed mission to Mars dies suddenly, backup Hattie Fredericks gets the coveted place on the crew. But her presence on the Starship provokes suspicion when it coincides with a series of incidents which threaten to derail the mission.

After a near-miss while landing on the planet, the world watches as Hattie and her fellow astronauts struggle to survive. But, worse than the harsh elements on Mars, is their growing realisation that someone, somewhere, is trying to destroy the mission.

When more astronauts die, Hattie doesn't know who to trust. And her only allies are 35 million miles away. As the tension ratchets up, violence and suspicion invade both worlds. If you like science-based sci-fi and a locked-room mystery with a twist, you'll love this book.

The Green Family Saga

Rebel Green – Book 1
Relationships fracture when two families find themselves caught up in the Irish Troubles.
The Green family move to Kilkenny from England in 1969, at the beginning of the conflict in Northern Ireland. They rent a farmhouse on the outskirts of town and make friends with the O'Connor family next door. Not every member of the family adapts easily to their new life, and their differing approaches lead to misunderstandings and friction. Despite this, the bonds between the family members deepen with time.

Perturbed by the worsening violence in the North threatening to invade their lives, the children make a pact never to let the troubles come between them. But promises can be broken, with tragic consequences for everyone.

Africa Green – Book 2
Will a white chimp save its rescuers or get them killed?
Journalist Isabella Green travels to Sierra Leone, a country emerging from civil war, to write an article about a chimp sanctuary. Animals that need saving are her obsession, and she can't resist getting involved with the project, which is on the verge of bankruptcy. She forms a bond with local boy, Ten, and army veteran, Pete, to try to save it. When they rescue a rare white chimp from a village frequented by a dangerous rebel splinter group, the resulting media interest could save the sanctuary. But the rebel group has not signed the ceasefire. They believe the voodoo power of the white chimp protects them from bullets, and they are determined to take it back so they can storm the capital.

When Pete and Ten go missing, only Isabella stands in the rebels' way. Her love for the chimps unlocks the fighting spirit within her. Can she save the sanctuary or will she die trying?

Fighting Green – Book 3
Liz Green is desperate for a change. The Dot-Com boom is raging in the City of London, and she feels exhausted and out of her depth. Added to that, her long-term boyfriend, Sean O'Connor, is drinking too much and shows signs of going off the rails. Determined to start anew, Liz abandons both Sean and her job, and buys a near-derelict house in Ireland to renovate.
She moves to Thomastown where she renews old ties and makes new ones, including two lawyers who become rivals for her affection. When Sean's attempt to win her back goes disastrously wrong, Liz finishes with him for good. Finding herself almost penniless, and forced to seek new ways to survive, Liz is torn between making a fresh start and going back to her old loves.
Can Liz make a go of her new life, or will her past become her future?

The Sam Harris Series (written as PJ Skinner)
Set in the late 1980s and through the 1990s, the thrilling Sam Harris Adventure series navigates through the career of a female geologist. Themes such as women working in formerly male domains, and what constitutes a normal existence, are developed in the context of Sam's constant ability to find herself in the middle of an adventure or mystery. Sam's home life provides a contrast to her adventures and feeds her

need to escape. Her attachment to an unfaithful boyfriend is the thread running through her romantic life, and her attempts to break free of it provide another side to her character.

The first book in the Sam Harris Series sets the scene for the career of an unwilling heroine, whose bravery and resourcefulness are needed to navigate a series of adventures set in remote sites in Africa and South America. Based loosely on the real-life adventures of the author, the settings and characters are given an authenticity that will connect with readers who enjoy adventure fiction and mysteries set in remote settings with realistic scenarios.

Fool's Gold - Book 1

Newly qualified geologist Sam Harris is a woman in a man's world - overlooked, underpaid but resilient and passionate. Desperate for her first job, and nursing a broken heart, she accepts an offer from notorious entrepreneur Mike Morton, to search for gold deposits in the remote rainforests of Sierramar. With the help of nutty local heiress Gloria Sanchez, she soon settles into life in Calderon, the capital. But when she accidentally uncovers a long-lost clue to a treasure buried deep within the jungle, her journey really begins. Teaming up with geologist Wilson Ortega, historian Alfredo Vargas and the mysterious Don Moises, they venture through the jungle, where she lurches between excitement and insecurity. Yet there is a far graver threat looming; Mike and Gloria discover that one member of the expedition is plotting to seize the fortune for himself and will do anything to get it. Can Sam survive and find the treasure, or will her first adventure be her last?

Hitler's Finger - Book 2
The second book in the Sam Harris Series sees the return of our heroine Sam Harris to Sierramar to help her friend Gloria track down her boyfriend, the historian Alfredo Vargas. Geologist Sam Harris loves getting her hands dirty. So, when she learns that her friend Alfredo has gone missing in Sierramar, she gives her personal life some much needed space and hops on the next plane. But she never expected to be following the trail of a devious Nazi plot nearly 50 years after World War II ... Deep in a remote mountain settlement, Sam must uncover the village's dark history. If she cannot reach her friend in time, the Nazi survivors will ensure Alfredo's permanent silence. Can Sam blow the lid on the conspiracy before the Third Reich makes a devastating return?

The Star of Simbako - Book 3
A fabled diamond, a jealous voodoo priestess, disturbing cultural practices. What might go wrong? The third book in the Sam Harris Series sees Sam Harris on her first contract to West Africa to Simbako, a land of tribal kingdoms and voodoo. Nursing a broken heart, Sam Harris goes to Simbako to work in the diamond fields of Fona. She is soon involved with a cast of characters who are starring in their own soap opera, a dangerous mix of superstition, cultural practices, and ignorance (mostly her own). Add a love triangle and a jealous woman who wants her dead and Sam is in trouble again. Where is the Star of Simbako? Is Sam going to survive the chaos?

The Pink Elephants - Book 4
Sam gets a call in the middle of the night that takes her to the Masaibu project in Lumbono, Africa. The

project is collapsing under the weight of corruption and chicanery engendered by management, both in country and back on the main company board. Sam has to navigate murky waters to get it back on course, not helped by interference from people who want her to fail. When poachers invade the elephant sanctuary next door, her problems multiply. Can Sam protect the elephants and save the project or will she have to choose?

The Bonita Protocol - Book 5
An erratic boss. Suspicious results. Stock market shenanigans. Can Sam Harris expose the scam before they silence her? It's 1996. Geologist Sam Harris has been around the block, but she's prone to nostalgia, so she snatches the chance to work in Sierramar, her old stomping ground. But she never expected to be working for a company that is breaking all the rules. When the analysis results from drill samples are suspiciously high, Sam makes a decision that puts her life in peril. Can she blow the lid on the conspiracy before they shut her up for good?

Digging Deeper - Book 6
A feisty geologist working in the diamond fields of West Africa is kidnapped by rebels. Can she survive the ordeal, or will this adventure be her last? It's 1998. Geologist Sam Harris is desperate for money, so she takes a job in a tinpot mining company working in war-torn Tamazia. But she never expected to be kidnapped by blood thirsty rebels.
Working in Gemsite would never be easy with its culture of misogyny and corruption. Her boss, the notorious Adrian Black is engaged in a game of cat and mouse with the government over taxation. Just when

Sam makes a breakthrough, the camp is overrun by rebels and Sam is taken captive. Will anyone bother to rescue her, and will she still be alive if they do?

<u>Concrete Jungle - Book 7</u> (series end)
Armed with an MBA, Sam Harris is storming the City - But has she swapped one jungle for another?
Forging a new career would never be easy, and Sam discovers she has not escaped from the culture of misogyny and corruption that blighted her field career. When her past is revealed, she finally achieves the acceptance she has always craved, but being one of the boys is not the panacea she expected. The death of a new friend presents her with the stark choice of compromising her principals to keep her new position, or exposing the truth behind the façade. Will she finally get what she wants or was it all a mirage?
Box Sets

Also Available
Sam Harris Adventure Box Set Book 2-4
Sam Harris Adventure Box Set Book 5-7
Sam Harris Adventure Box Set Books 2-7

Connect with the Author

I write under several pen names and in various genres: PJ Skinner (Travel Adventures and Cozy/Cosy Mystery), Pip Skinner (Sci-Fi), Kate Foley (Irish contemporary), and Jessica Parkin (children's illustrated books).

When I moved to the south coast of England just before the Covid pandemic and after finishing my trilogy, The Green Family Saga, I planned the Seacastle Mysteries. I have always been a massive fan of crime and mystery and I guess it was inevitable I would turn my hand to a mystery series eventually.

Before I wrote novels, I spent 30 years working as an exploration geologist, managing remote sites and doing due diligence of projects in over thirty countries. During this time, I collected the tall tales and real-life experiences which inspired the Sam Harris Adventure Series, chronicling the adventures of a female geologist as a pioneer in a hitherto exclusively male world.

My childhood in Ireland inspired me to write the Green Family Saga, which follows the fortunes of an English family who move to Ireland just before the start of the troubles.

I have also written a mystery on Mars, inspired by my fascination with all things celestial. It is a science-based murder mystery, think The Martian with fewer potatoes and more bodies.

Please subscribe to my Seacastle Mysteries Newsletter for updates and offers by using this QR code

You can also use the QR code below to get to my website for updates and to buy paperbacks direct from me.

You can also follow me on Twitter, Instagram or on Facebook @pjskinnerauthor

Printed in Dunstable, United Kingdom